THE BADGE: BOOK 15

★

# FARRELL'S WAR

★

## Bill Reno

**TM** **BCI**  Created by the producers of
**Wagons West, White Indian,
Stagecoach,** and **Abilene.**

*Book Creations Inc., Canaan, NY · Lyle Kenyon Engel, Founder*

**BANTAM BOOKS**
NEW YORK · TORONTO · LONDON · SYDNEY · AUCKLAND

FARRELL'S WAR
*A Bantam Book / Book Creations, Inc.*
*Bantam edition / February 1990*

*Produced by Book Creations, Inc.*
*Lyle Kenyon Engel, Founder*

ISBN 0-553-28342-1

*Published simultaneously in the United States and Canada*

Bantam Books are published by Bantam Books, a division of
Bantam Doubleday Dell Publishing Group, Inc. Its trademark,
consisting of the words "Bantam Books" and the portrayal of a
rooster, is Registered in U.S. Patent and Trademark Office and
in other countries. Marca Registrada. Bantam Books, 666 Fifth
Avenue, New York, New York 10103.

PRINTED IN THE UNITED STATES OF AMERICA

OPM      0 9 8 7 6 5 4 3 2 1

# FARRELL'S WAR

# BADGE

So important was the buffalo to the Indians' way of life that they considered it a sacred animal. They used every part of the beast—for food, shelter, tools, and recreation—except the heart, which was always left behind in the belief that it would help the herd to regenerate.

Before whites arrived, the buffalo population was about 75 million; by 1900 it was down to about 1,000. White hunters were more efficient than the Indians, each man killing as many as 150 animals in a day. Often they would leave the meat to rot after skinning the animals. Today, approximately 10,000 buffalo exist on game preserves.

© BOOK CREATIONS INC. 1989          R. TOELKE '89

## Book 15: Farrell's War

# Chapter One

The morning sun cast a barred shadow on the floor of the cell as Sheriff Tug Farrell entered, carrying the limp form of Kyle Fox over his powerful shoulder. Crossing the small space, he eased the unconscious man onto the bunk. Dr. Fred Halsey, black satchel in hand, came in right behind the sheriff.

"Okay, Tug," the elderly physician said with a dismissive wave, "stand back and let me work."

Standing with his hands on his hips, Farrell stepped away from the bunk but kept a close watch on his unconscious prisoner as the doctor labored to stop the flow of blood oozing from a deep cut on Fox's temple.

After a few moments Halsey mumbled, "I take back that order. I'll have to stitch him up. Come over here and hold his head so's he doesn't move it when I stab him with the needle."

Farrell stepped back to the cot and with his powerful hands grasped Fox's jaws, holding him tight. Halsey then hurriedly pulled the split skin together with needle and thread, grunting, "Son, you really clobbered him. He's still out cold."

"It's better than being dead, wouldn't you say?" remarked Farrell in a wry voice. "It was kill him or clobber him. I chose the latter."

Without looking away from his task, the physician asked, "May I ask why?"

"Sure. I figured you needed the business more than the undertaker did."

The elderly physician's mouth worked into a slow grin. Still concentrating on his task, Halsey chuckled, then commented, "You know darn well what I mean. Why did you take the chance of rushing to him and hitting him with your gun when you could have drawn that Colt and killed him with it in the twinkling of an eye? After all, if he'd been a mite faster, he'd have plugged you before you got to him."

Kyle Fox began to stir. He moaned and tried to move his head, but it was held fast by the tall, muscular lawman. Responding to the doctor's comments, Farrell said, "Strange as it may sound coming from a man who's put twenty-nine men in their graves, I hate killing. Even a fool who rides into this town thinking he's going to be the one to outdraw Tug Farrell won't be put down by me unless I have to do it."

"But, Tug, I say again, you could've taken a bullet before you closed the gap between the two of you."

"I have to kill too many men in this job as it is. I feel good when I can keep some fool from dying uselessly. Like Fox, here. Maybe the terrible headache he's going to have will make him give up the idea of trying to engrave his name in the history books as a great gun-fighter."

The injured man suddenly opened his eyes and looked sharply first at Farrell, then at Halsey.

"Just lie still, Mr. Fox," the doctor said softly. "I'm almost finished."

Fox licked his lips and blinked, as if trying to clear away a fog. Finally finding his voice, he swore at the lawman, declaring, "You yellow-bellied coward! You didn't have the guts to draw against me! Had to whack me one, instead! Just wait'll I'm outta here!"

Fred Halsey closed his medical bag with a loud snap, and cautioned, "Let me tell you, Mr. Fox, Tug Farrell could draw and fire six times while you're still hunting for your holster. I was standing there when you challenged him, and it was mighty good advice when he told you to get on your horse and ride. But you just had to go for your gun, didn't you? Look, you dumb fool, he reached your side and conked you on the noggin while you were just clearing leather. Don't you think he could have drawn and killed you a whole lot faster than it took him to close the distance between you? You're plenty lucky to be alive—and you should be thanking the sheriff, not challenging him again."

Fox glared at the physician for a moment, but it was clear that the words had registered. He looked away, mumbling, "I'll show you."

The lawman released his prisoner and backed toward the cell door, shaking his head. "Well, that attitude's not going to help you. I'll tell you what, Fox, until you get that fool notion out of your head, you're not leaving this jail. Let's go, Doc."

Swearing vehemently, Kyle Fox pushed himself up to a sitting position as the two men left the cell and the door clanged shut. "You ain't got no reason to hold me in this jail, Farrell!" he shouted after the lawman's retreating back. "I demand you let me outta here! Right now!"

Farrell and Halsey were almost to the office door when the big sheriff halted, turned around, and walked back to the cell. His eyes blazing, he snapped, "Mr. Fox, you don't demand anything of me, you hear? I'll let you out when you're ready to leave Denver for good. As for now, I'd advise you to cool down." The sheriff started to turn away, but then he looked back at Fox and said, "By the way, you owe Doc for the stitching job. Fork over twenty-five dollars."

Fox's mouth flew open. "Twenty-five dollars! That's robbery! Ain't no doctor charges that kind of dough for sewin' up a cut! Why, that's all the money I got on me, for cryin' out loud!"

Fred Halsey stepped beside the sheriff and murmured, "Tug, that *is* awfully high. Five dollars will more than cover it."

"I say he owes you twenty-five," insisted Farrell. Sticking his hand through the bars, he demanded, "Now, Fox. Now!"

It was evident from the expression on the lawman's

face that he would not accept any excuse, and one way or the other, Kyle Fox was going to pay Dr. Fred Halsey twenty-five dollars for stitching up his head. Reaching into his pocket, the prisoner produced the designated amount and laid it in Farrell's hand, muttering under his breath.

"Thank you," the sheriff said with exaggerated politeness, handing the money to Halsey.

As the two men headed for the office again, Fox yelled, "I want outta here, Farrell!"

Speaking over his shoulder without breaking his stride, Farrell told his prisoner, "Cool off, mister, and we'll talk about it."

When the door to the cell area was closed behind them, Halsey looked at the wad of bills in his hand and said, "Tug, I can't take this much for what I just did."

"Sure you can," Farrell countered, chuckling. "Like I said, it was you or the undertaker, and I thought you could use the business."

Halsey shrugged, stuffed the money in a pocket, and headed for the door. "See you later."

Before the physician could touch the knob, the door opened, and seventy-eight-year-old Maynard Farrell, the sheriff's father, entered the office. The old gentleman's second wife had died recently, and he had come from Missouri to Denver to live with his son, whom he had not seen in a number of years.

Maynard's back was bent from the years that were upon him, and his silver hair was growing thin, but there was still a sparkle in his sky-blue eyes. As Maynard Farrell and the physician belonged to the same generation, they had become fast friends, and Maynard's weathered, leathery face split into a crooked grin when he saw Halsey. Pushing back the old hat that he refused to give up, he cackled, " 'Mornin', Fred. I didn't know you ever got outta bed this early."

Halsey squinted and parried, "Why, you old coot. I was out of bed while you were still under the covers dreaming about being as handsome as I am."

"Hah!" barked Maynard. "You wouldn't know what handsome was if you saw it!"

His eyes running from the elderly Farrell's battered hat to his split, cracked boots, Halsey chortled, "I suppose you think that mangled Stetson and those petrified boots are handsome!"

"Well, I suppose it takes an old fossil to recognize somethin' petrified."

"Okay, you two," cut in Tug, trying hard to sound stern, but laughing instead, "that's enough. Hush it up right now, or I'll jail both of you!"

Maynard elbowed his friend and declared, "The kid's gettin' purty big for his britches, Doc. Which one of us is gonna take him down a peg or two?"

"It'll have to be you this time," replied the aging physician. "I've got business to tend to. See you later. 'Bye, Tug."

When the door closed behind Halsey, the sheriff remarked, "You know, Pop, Doc's right about that hat and those boots. You really ought to—"

"We've discussed this subject before, son," Maynard cut in, raising a palm toward his offspring, "and it ain't gonna do no good to discuss it again. You can get me into new pants, shirt, and underwear, but when it comes to my hat and my boots, you've got a fight on your hands!"

The lawman merely threw up his hands, accepting defeat.

"That's better," his father quipped. "Now. New subject. I hear you about knocked some dude's head clean off a little while ago."

Sighing, the sheriff admitted, "Yeah. It seemed the better thing to do than killing him."

Maynard snorted. "When are these boneheads gonna learn that there ain't a man alive who can match you in *any* kind of a fight?"

Tug Farrell lowered his head and stroked his well-trimmed mustache. "I think you've placed me a little higher on the hero scale than I really am, Pop."

The old man grinned. "Ah, I'm glad to see that your

mama and I raised you right and instilled humbleness and humility in you." He turned toward the door. "Anyway, I just thought I'd drop by, bless you with my presence for a minute, and see if you was all right."

"I'm just fine, Pop," the younger man promised. "You run along and enjoy this fine day. It's almost October, which means we won't have too many more mild days like this one before the snow starts piling up fast and·furious out there."

"So you keep warnin' me," Maynard said. "I guess it'll take some adjustin' to, after Missouri. Well, see you later."

The oldster left the office, and the lawman returned to his desk. Denver County's sheriff was a powerful and ruggedly handsome man well over six feet tall. As tough as cured rawhide, he was doggedly determined to maintain law and order in his county, and his far-flung reputation did not exaggerate his ability to subdue a wrongdoer with either his fists or his fast draw. A widower for some time, at thirty-seven Tug Farrell had long felt that his job was his life.

Sinking into his chair, Farrell reached for the stack of mail and sifted through it. He was slitting an envelope when the door came open, and he looked up to see his youthful deputy, Harlon Stang. Glancing at the clock on the wall, Farrell commented, "It's five minutes after eight, Mr. Stang. You're late."

Crossing the room, his face clouded with worry, the deputy held up a newspaper. "This will explain my tardiness," he announced, laying the *Rocky Mountain Sentinel* on his boss's desk.

The sheriff's eyes automatically scanned the date, September 30, 1877, and then he read the bold headline underneath the masthead: "GOVERNOR PREVIOUSLY JAILED FOR EMBEZZLEMENT." The lead article, which took up the entire front page and continued inside, told of Colorado Governor Stephen Harrison's having been imprisoned in Maryland years earlier for embezzlement before changing his name and coming west. Written by Charles Duncan, publisher and man-

aging editor of the *Sentinel,* the article revealed that
the governor's real name was George Harris, and two
photographs on page three proved that Harris and Harrison were the same man.

Duncan's article asserted that George Harris had
embezzled some forty thousand dollars from a law firm
in which he was a partner. After serving seven years in
prison, he had been paroled, and shortly thereafter,
Harris, his wife, Clara, and their five sons had disappeared from their home state. The documented evidence showed that Harris changed his name, falsified
his law degree with the new name, and set up a law
office in Denver in May 1872. Winning the hearts of his
fellow citizens, along with numerous cases, he had been
trusted so implicitly by the people of Colorado that they
made him their governor when the territory became a
state in 1876.

Tug Farrell was completely shaken by the news. He
stood and grabbed his hat, then shoved it on, instructing
his deputy, "Watch the office, Harlon. I'm going over to
see Charlie Duncan." Grabbing the newspaper, he
bolted through the doorway.

The big sheriff hurried down the street toward the
*Sentinel* office. As he neared his destination, he saw
the short and stout middle-aged publisher standing at
the window, thoughtfully tugging on his handlebar
mustache as he watched his fellow citizens speaking
animatedly with one another. Charles Duncan spied
Tug Farrell in turn, and when the lawman opened the
door, Duncan was standing there to meet him.

Holding the rolled-up newspaper at eye level, the
sheriff declared, "Charlie, I know your paper stood
against the governor in the election, but this stuff is
dynamite. I hope you haven't bitten off more than you
can chew."

Duncan shrugged and responded, "The truth's the
truth, Tug. It's my job to seek it out, and it's my job to
print it."

"You're sure you've got all the facts straight in this
article?"

"I've been in the newspaper business a long time, Tug, and I wouldn't have printed that story if it weren't absolutely true," Duncan assured him. "I've had a gut feeling about Harrison since before he ran for governor. It kept nagging at me, so I decided to check him out. I started working on this back in the spring, doing some probing through my newspaper contacts back East, and all the information came together about two weeks ago. So you see, I've taken a good long while to carefully assemble my facts before being certain they were ready to print."

Glancing away from the publisher, Farrell noticed that although Duncan's employees were ostensibly busy at the printing press and the typesetting table, they were straining their ears to pick up every word of the conversation. Looking down at Duncan again, the lawman asked, "Charlie, did you talk to Harrison about this discovery of yours before putting it to press?"

Shaking his head emphatically, Duncan replied, "Absolutely not! Like I said, my job is to seek out the truth and print it. I've done that. Harrison became governor under false pretenses—and now he'll have to suffer the consequences."

"Have you thought about how Harrison's five sons will take this?" the sheriff asked with concern. "Mind you, I wouldn't want you to cover for anybody, Charlie, but you'd better be ready for trouble. I've got a feeling those boys won't take this sitting down."

The governor's five sons, who jointly owned a cattle ranch about ten miles east of Denver, were a hotheaded bunch—especially the oldest son, David, and the youngest, Olan, who had caused trouble in the past when they came into town carousing. In fact, Farrell had found it necessary to jail the twosome on more than one occasion. Though Gordon, Harold, and Rick Harrison were also hot-tempered, at least they were levelheaded enough not to tangle with Farrell, and when he told them to get on their horses and go home, they did so, even though they were tanked up on whiskey.

Duncan tugged at his handlebar mustache again

and sighed. "Yes, I've thought about the boys. Things could get sticky, I guess, but I can't suppress the truth for anybody's sake—not even my own." Looking the lawman in the eye, he added, "It's my job to print the facts, Tug. It's your job to protect Denver's citizens from troublemakers."

"I'll do my best," Farrell assured him, reaching for the doorknob, "but you'd best glance over your shoulder once in a while. I'm only one man—and there are five of them. You might just get a visit from the governor, too."

"I'm ready," responded Duncan.

The street was buzzing with conversation as the lawman walked back to his office, and the topic on everyone's lips was the same: the disclosure about the governor. People were huddled together in small groups, excitedly waving copies of the morning edition of the newspaper and offering their opinions, and Farrell was stopped several times by his fellow townsmen to give his views. Finally reaching his office, the sheriff entered and found Deputy Harlon Stang discussing the situation with Town Council Chairman Wilbur Bonds.

The councilman shook his head slowly and declared, "Well, Tug, looks like we've got a hot one going, eh?"

"You sure might say that," Farrell agreed.

"Harlon said you were having a talk with Charlie," Bonds continued. "Are you going to talk to Harrison too?"

"Don't see any need to," responded Farrell. "It's not a situation needing a sheriff. Charlie seems to have irrefutable proof about everything he printed. Nature will simply have to take its course."

"I'll tell you what that will be," Bonds asserted. "The Colorado legislature will call an emergency meeting and demand Harrison's resignation."

"Without a doubt," agreed the lawman.

"Well, it makes me sick," growled Bonds. "I mean, the way Harrison pulled the wool over our eyes like that. It's a crying shame when people put their faith in a man, and then he turns out to be a lying scoundrel."

With a final disgusted mutter, the councilman tossed his copy of the paper on the desk and left the office.

"I should be heading off, too," Harlon Stang announced. "You wanted me to run those errands for you."

"Yeah, thanks," Farrell responded in a distracted tone, his mind still on the governor.

Stang closed the door behind him, and with the office quiet and empty, Tug Farrell sat down at his desk and shoved the newspaper to the side, then picked up the stack of mail again. But he found himself unable to concentrate on the task and, giving up, he tossed aside the mail and picked up the newspaper. Opening the newspaper to page three, he studied the two photographs, shaking his head in disbelief. The governor was a crook, all right.

Suddenly Farrell's eye caught a small headline on the lower part of the page, announcing the capture of a couple on charges of kidnapping and slave labor. The article related that a man and a woman—who had been arrested near Sacramento, California, by Sheriff Bob Sovern—had found a vein of gold in the Sierra Nevada mountains east of Sacramento that had been overlooked in the gold rush of 1849. After assembling a gang of hoodlums and setting up a mining camp, the pair organized the kidnapping of local men and forced them to work the mine. Sheriff Sovern related that the gang was headed up by an attractive brunette in her late twenties named Rita Marston. Her partner, Clarence Hoffman, was in his mid-thirties.

Farrell dropped the newspaper on the desk and rubbed his temples, his thoughts racing back three years to the slave mine he had broken up in a Rocky Mountain canyon several miles west of Denver. Beautiful brunette Raven Morrow and her henchman, Clete Hobbs—who coincidentally fitted the description of the couple now incarcerated at the Sacramento County jail

—had run the mine, and a number of kidnapped men had died for their nefarious scheme.

Troubled by the memories, Farrell stood and walked to the window at the front of the office. Digging his hands into his pockets, he stared blankly, unaware of all the activity outside. The coincidence was indeed uncanny, Farrell decided, but that was all it was—a coincidence. The vile pair were dead, having died in the mine while attempting to elude Farrell through a specially prepared escape shaft. Dynamite stored near the bottom of the shaft had caught fire and exploded, trapping Raven and Hobbs in the shaft. If they had not been killed immediately by tons of falling rock, they died soon thereafter because all their escape routes had been sealed by that same rubble.

Returning to the desk, the sheriff read the article again. *Absolutely amazing,* he thought. *Method of operation, ages, descriptions . . . But those two have been dead for three years. Their bodies are buried in the bowels of that mountain. They—*

The sheriff's thoughts were interrupted as the door came open, revealing two more councilmen wanting to discuss the incredible news about the governor. Farrell invited them to sit down, and his mind was once again on the main subject of conversation on the lips of every citizen in Denver.

In the big mansion just east of Denver's business district, Governor Stephen Harrison was shaving in his bathroom on the second floor while his wife, Clara, was combing her hair at her dressing table in their large bedroom. At the sound of the light tap on the bedroom door, Clara pulled her robe tight around her and went to respond. Pulling the door open, she asked the young maid standing there, "What is it, Pauline?"

"I'm sorry to bother you so early, ma'am," the maid replied in an apologetic tone, "but Mr. Vine is here. He seems quite upset and wants to see the governor at once."

Clara was surprised. "My husband's top aide certainly knows the governor's schedule," she mused, half aloud and half to herself. "I wonder what's so important that it can't wait until he goes to his office." In a more forthright voice she declared, "Tell Mr. Vine the governor will be down shortly, Pauline."

The governor's wife then closed the door and hurried across the room to the bathroom. Looking at her husband's reflection in the mirror over the sink, she told him, "Darling, Tom Vine is here. Pauline said he's upset and wants to see you immediately."

The governor, his face half-covered with shaving soap, scowled. "I've told my people not to bother me at home unless it's a matter of life and death."

"Tom is a good man, darling, and he certainly knows your feelings about this," Clara said soothingly. "This can only mean that it must be extremely important. I'll go down and keep him company. Hurry, will you?"

Padding back across the room and out to the landing, Clara Harrison descended the winding staircase and greeted Thomas Vine. Although he did not reveal what he had come for, it was obvious that he was very disturbed.

Moments later, the governor came down, also clad in a robe, his hair not yet combed. His face petulant, he eyed his aide and snapped, "This better be awfully important, Tom! What is it?"

Vine's expression hovered between fear and dismay. "I . . . I have to ask you a question, Governor," he said, holding a rolled-up newspaper in a shaky hand.

"Well, out with it!" lashed Harrison.

"Is . . . is your real name George Harris?"

Clara gasped, and her hand went to her mouth, but while the governor's eyes clearly showed his shock, his face was as stony as granite. "Why would you ask me such a question?" he spat.

Ignoring the question, Vine asked another. "Did you spend seven years in prison in Maryland for embezzlement?"

Clara's eyes filled with tears, and she began to

shake. An angry frown flickered across Harrison's brow, and he rasped, "Clara! Get a hold on yourself!" Then, turning to Vine, he declared, "My name is not George Harris, and I've never been in prison! Where are you getting such ideas?"

Without a word, Thomas Vine unrolled the morning edition of the *Rocky Mountain Sentinel,* exposing the front page to the governor, and placed it in his hand. As the governor silently read the article, his hands began to tremble and, reading to the bottom of the page, he flipped it to page three with a jerk. When he saw the two pictures of himself, he closed the paper and handed it back to Vine.

Harrison's face was that of a haunted man. He stared at his wife, who stood crying softly, for a long moment. Then, without a word, the governor turned and slowly climbed the stairs, his footsteps making no noise on the thickly carpeted treads.

The huge house was silent except for Clara's soft weeping. Then from overhead came the sound of the bedroom door closing.

The sound seemed to release the young maid from her shocked daze. Leaving her post by the door, she dashed to Clara Harrison and murmured, "I'm sorry, ma'am. Truly sorry. May I get you something?"

"A little water would help, Pauline, thank you," Clara whispered.

As the maid hurried to the kitchen, Vine took Clara's hand and told her, "Come, you need to sit down."

The aide guided the governor's wife into the parlor and eased her down on an overstuffed couch. He then handed her his handkerchief. Clara dabbed at her face and her nose, then drew a shuddering breath and said, "This will finish him, Tom. I don't know what will happen to us now." She sighed, then moaned, "Somebody must ride out and tell the boys. Their father is going to need them."

Vine assured Clara, "I'll ride out to the ranch right

now, Mrs. Harrison. I'm sure it will help the governor to have his sons with him."

Pauline returned with a glass of water, and Clara took it and sipped slowly. Handing the glass back to the maid, the governor's wife rose from the couch, lifted her head high, and told the aide, "My place is by my husband's side. Pauline will see you out."

Clara Harrison was starting toward the staircase when the sound of a gunshot rang out from the second floor and reverberated through the mansion. Clara screamed, her cry of horror weaving in with the echoing sound of the shot. Then she collapsed on the floor.

# Chapter Two

Sheriff Tug Farrell was alone in his office, reading the last piece of mail, when the door was flung open and Wilbur Bonds burst into the room as if he had been blown by a high wind. "Tug!" the council chairman gasped. "The governor just shot himself!"

Farrell jumped to his feet and clapped on his hat. "Is he dead?"

"Yes. Put a bullet right through his brain. Doc Halsey's already over there."

Farrell mumbled a response and bolted for the door.

"What'd you say?" called Bonds, following on the lawman's heels.

Running ahead of him, the sheriff yelled back over his shoulder, "I said I was afraid of something like this happening!"

Farrell's long-legged strides soon left Wilbur Bonds far behind. As he ran toward Grant Street, where the governor's mansion was situated, the sheriff felt a cold ball of fear settling in his stomach. The governor's suicide was bound to be the catalyst for more trouble. Harrison's five sons would seek vengeance on Charlie Duncan, sure as anything.

After sprinting four blocks, Farrell made a right turn onto Grant Street, then stopped, breathing hard. A small crowd had collected on the street in front of the mansion, while parked in tandem on the house's circular drive were Doc Halsey's buggy and the undertaker's hearse. Standing at the mansion's front door in conversation with the governor's young maid was Charlie Duncan.

Making his way across the street, the sheriff pushed through the crowd and hurried up the front steps. At the same instant, the conversation between the maid and the newspaper publisher halted as the undertaker and his helper came through the doorway carrying a stretcher. The lifeless form on the stretcher was covered completely with a blanket.

The undertaker looked at Farrell and muttered, "Brains all over the bedroom, Tug. I mean *all over.*"

Farrell nodded and let them pass. As soon as they had cleared the doorway, Duncan turned back to the maid, telling her insistently, "Come on, Pauline. All I need is a few minutes to get a statement from Mrs. Harrison."

Clearly bitter, the young woman retorted scornfully, "Haven't you done enough damage for one day, Mr. Duncan? Mrs. Harrison is in shock. I'm sure Dr. Halsey, who is with her at this moment, would not permit such an intrusion. I repeat: You are not going in there!"

Pauline glanced at the lawman, and he read the pleading look in her eyes. Putting a firm hand on the newspaperman's shoulder, Farrell said sharply, "Charlie, have you taken leave of your senses? Mrs. Harrison's husband was just carried out of here with his brains blown out. She's in no condition to give you a statement, and you're undoubtedly the last man on earth she wants to see."

Pauline shot Duncan a hot look, then remarked, "You might have had the decency to discuss your damaging information with the governor before you printed it, giving him the opportunity to quietly resign and move away. It's your fault he took his own life."

Anger flared on the face of the stout little publisher. "Hold it a minute, missy!" he blustered. "The man was a scoundrel! If he hadn't manufactured that can of worms, there wouldn't have been one for me to open! That he couldn't face the world after his deception was exposed isn't any fault of mine!"

Pauline drew a sharp breath, clearly ready to spew back some tart words, but Tug Farrell broke in, "Charlie, that's enough!"

The publisher glared up at the sheriff for a moment. Then, pivoting, he brushed past Farrell down the steps and headed up the street. The sheriff watched him till he was out of sight, then turned back to the maid.

"You look a little peaked," he remarked in a soft voice. "Why don't we go inside so you can sit down?"

Pauline nodded, preceding him into the hallway, then closing the door behind him. She led him the way to the parlor, and they both sat down.

Looking at the maid, Farrell asked, "Has anyone gone to the ranch to advise the boys?"

"Yes. Mr. Vine, the governor's aide, left right after it happened. They should be returning in another quarter-hour or so."

Farrell made up his mind to remain there until the Harrison brothers arrived. If they showed any inclination toward getting even with Charlie Duncan, he wanted to be there to ward them off.

Thomas Vine stood in the kitchen of the big ranch house with his hat in his hand as David Harrison, at twenty-nine the oldest son, paced back and forth, shaking the newspaper while swearing vehemently. Gordon, Harold, and Rick sat in numb disbelief, their eyes fixed on the floor, as they waited for their youngest brother, Olan, to arrive. Two of the ranch hands had ridden out to find him on the range.

"Duncan's gonna pay for this!" rasped David, rattling the paper. "He's gonna pay dearly!" He had been repeating the threat over and over since the governor's aide first arrived and broke the dreadful news.

Gordon, the second oldest of the brothers, sighed and stood up. "David, you've got to cool down."

David stopped and looked at Gordon incredulously. "Cool down? What do you mean, cool down?

That scoundrel caused Dad to blow his brains out! He's gonna pay, I tell you!"

Gordon stepped close to David, his face inches away from his brother's, and warned, "If you're carrying on like this when Olan shows up, you'll only fuel his fire. You know he's got a hair-trigger temper. When he sees that newspaper and finds out what Dad did, he'll want to ride into town and kill Duncan on the spot!"

"What's so terrible about that?" David countered.

Gordon ran shaky fingers through his dark hair and shook his head. "Look, I'm as angry about what Duncan did as you are, but Olan or you killing the man isn't gonna bring Dad back. It'll only put a rope around your necks—which sure won't give Mother the support she needs."

At that moment the kitchen door flew open and Olan Harrison entered. He gazed questioningly at each of his brothers, then turned to Thomas Vine. "What's going on?" he asked. "The guys who came after me said it was something serious, but they didn't know what."

"We've got to get into town quick," spoke up Gordon. "Mother needs us."

"Why?"

"Because Dad's dead," came the gloomy reply. "He killed himself this morning."

Olan's mouth sagged, and he stared blankly at his brother for a long moment, as if not really hearing what had been said. Finally he stammered, "He . . . he killed himself? Why? What for? What happened?"

David shoved the newspaper into his brother's hand, then let Thomas Vine tell Olan of the events that had led up to his father's suicide.

Olan went into a rage, both weeping and swearing as the mixed feelings of grief and wrath tumbled inside him. The twenty-year-old shook both fists and screamed, "I'm gonna kill Duncan! I'm gonna kill him!"

David said, "I felt the same way, but Gordon's right. We won't be helping Mother by getting ourselves hanged. Don't worry. We'll take care of Charlie Duncan, all right—but not by killing him. We'll beat him to a pulp and burn down his building, preventing him from printing any more trash."

Harold and Rick both spoke up, agreeing with David that killing Duncan would not bring their father back and would only cause more grief for their mother. After several minutes, Olan listened to reason and quieted down, and then the five Harrison brothers and Thomas Vine mounted up and headed for Denver.

Reaching town, they slowed to a walk and guided their mounts down the main street toward Grant Street. They were nearing the center of town when they caught sight of Charles Duncan's portly form on the boardwalk, heading for his office.

Olan pointed down the street, growling, "Look, it's Duncan!" As he spoke he spurred his horse. Then his brothers immediately followed suit.

Charlie Duncan turned at the sound of the galloping hooves, and his expression instantly turned to one of horror as Olan Harrison headed directly toward him. At first the portly man merely threw up his hands as if trying to ward off his pursuer; then he tried to run for the safety of his office. But young Harrison skidded his horse to a halt directly in front of him, blocking his way. Duncan broke into a sweat and attempted repeatedly to go around the horse, but Olan kept reining the animal around, preventing the publisher's escape.

The other Harrison brothers came up alongside Olan, and David angrily warned him, "I told you, we'll deal with Duncan later. Right now we need to get to Mother."

Cursing loudly, the young hothead told his brother, "I'll tell you what I've got to do right now—make this scum newspaperman pay with his life!"

A crowd began to gather. Having heard the commotion from around the corner at the mansion, Sheriff Tug Farrell came dashing toward the scene as the argument between Olan and his brothers grew more heated. Charles Duncan, his face wet with perspiration and his body quaking with terror, tried to slip away, but young Harrison spotted him. Whipping out his revolver, Olan rose up in his stirrups, aimed, and squeezed the trigger. The revolver bucked against his palm and the bullet tore into Duncan's head.

A horrified gasp rose from the crowd. The four other Harrison brothers scrambled off their horses and knelt beside Charles Duncan's body. Gordon rose slowly to his feet, looked at Olan in disbelief, and screamed, "You fool! Now you'll hang!"

"You're probably right—although it'll be up to a judge to decide," Tug Farrell yelled from across the street. Walking toward Olan Harrison, the lawman shouted, "You're under arrest for the murder of Charles Duncan. Hand over your gun and get down off your horse."

Defiance was written all over young Harrison's face. Pulling hard on the reins, he began backing up his horse, preparing for flight. "No one takes my gun, Sheriff! Not even you!"

The sheriff's voice was harsh as he repeated, "Give me the gun and get off the horse!"

But instead of complying, the young man raised his revolver and fired. The bullet whipped off the sheriff's hat, and Farrell immediately reacted by drawing his own weapon and drilling Olan Harrison through the heart.

Young Harrison reeled out of the saddle, already dead by the time he hit the ground. Gordon, Harold, and Rick stood rooted in place as if frozen and unable to walk the half-dozen paces to their brother's lifeless body.

David dashed to Olan and stood over him, staring down at the sightless eyes. Pivoting, David glared at the lawman, his face filled with hate. "You didn't have to kill him, Farrell!" he snarled. "You could've winged him!"

Dropping his gun into its holster, Farrell retorted coldly, "When a man tries to kill me, he'd best be prepared to die, 'cause I'm going to defend myself."

David Harrison bristled and opened his mouth, but before he could say more, his brother Gordon called loudly, "David, that's enough! The sheriff did what he had to do. You saw it, just like the rest of us did. Olan tried to kill him!"

Ignoring his brother, David said heatedly to Tug Farrell, "He was just a kid—a twenty-year-old boy!"

Farrell snapped back, "That *boy* just murdered Charlie Duncan—and he tried to murder me! He'd have stretched a rope anyway!"

Blind with rage, David cursed Farrell and clawed for his gun.

"No, David!" Gordon screamed. "There's been enough bloodshed! Killing the sheriff will only cause Mother more grief!"

But David's hand would not be stayed, and he raised the gun. Tug Farrell went for his own weapon, drawing it with lightning speed, and the air was split by a double roar as Farrell's gun fired first, then David's. The lawman's bullet hit its target before the younger man brought his revolver to bear. While his bullet chewed dirt, David Harrison grabbed his chest with his free hand. Staggering three steps, his legs gave way, collapsing under him, and he sprawled facedown in the street.

Tug Farrell turned to the remaining Harrison brothers and stared wordlessly at them. But none of them attempted any retaliation. Finally Gordon asked in a small voice, "Sheriff, will you have the undertaker pick up their bodies? We've got to get to Mother before she learns of this." His voice quavered as he added, "I don't know how she's going to cope."

Holstering his gun, Farrell nodded. "I'll see they're taken care of, Gordon." He paused, then murmured, "I'm real sorry, son. I sure didn't want anything like this to happen."

His eyes downcast, Gordon responded, "I know. It wasn't your fault. You warned them fair."

No one in the crowd moved until the three Harrison brothers, accompanied by Thomas Vine, had turned the corner toward Grant Street and were out of earshot. The first to break the silence was Maynard Farrell, who hurried to his son as he picked up the bullet-torn hat. "I'm proud of the way you handled that situation, my boy. You did your best to keep them hot-heads from gettin' killed—it's just too bad they didn't listen." Turning to the rest of the onlookers, the old man said, "See? It don't make no difference how many bad dudes try to take on my son. They always find out they got a war on their hands!"

An hour later, Tug Farrell was back at his desk when the door to his office opened and three men came in. Tensing, Farrell looked up, then smiled broadly. He got to his feet and greeted the government agents familiarly. The tallest of the trio, Clyde Towner, was chief United States marshal in charge of the Denver office, and the two shorter men were special government agents Webster Richards and Donald Ingram.

"Got time to chat a few minutes?" asked Towner.

"Sure." Farrell nodded toward three chairs against the wall. "Grab a seat, gentlemen."

The federal men pulled the chairs over and sat in front of the desk. Farrell took his seat, then leaned across the desk and inquired, "What can I do for you, fellas?"

Towner, flanked by Richards and Ingram, shifted slightly and cleared his throat. Meeting Farrell's steady gaze, he replied, "Tug, we were in the crowd before when you faced down the Harrison brothers. Now, Web and I have observed your proficiency as a lawman ever since you've been our sheriff, and while Don's only been in Denver ten months, he's in complete agreement with us."

"About what?" Farrell asked.

"We think your talents and abilities could be put to better use than as sheriff of Denver County."

Farrell leaned back in his chair without comment and waited for Towner to proceed.

"I've seen you go up against outlaws in all kinds of situations," Towner went on. "You handle a gun like no man I've ever laid eyes on. You've got iron nerves and courage beyond anything I've ever seen."

Shaking his head in protest, Farrell declared, "Clyde, you're embarrassing me."

Towner laughed. "Be as modest as you like, Tug, but you've got some rare talents. Like your unique ability to track down criminals so they can be brought to justice. Why, I've never known anyone other than an Indian who can trail a man like you can."

Farrell rubbed his square jaw and quipped, "All right, fellas, I'm really impressed with myself. Now, what's all this flowery stuff leading up to?"

Clyde Towner leaned forward on his chair and replied, "We want you to put on a United States marshal's badge, Tug. The government needs men like you investigating federal crimes and hunting down outlaws."

The sheriff picked up a pencil and toyed with it. Smiling, he said, "I once thought about becoming a federal lawman, but not now."

"Tug," Towner put in, "don't be too hasty turning this down. More and more people are moving west—meaning more unsavory types are emigrating, too. There's an urgent need for more federal marshals—especially men of your caliber."

"Yeah," put in Webster Richards, "how many men would've found that hidden mining operation three years ago? And who knows how many more men would have been worked to death as slaves in that mine if you hadn't put a stop to it."

"That's right," agreed Clyde Towner. "There must have been a dozen other lawmen, including some federals, who tried to find that mine and shut it down. It took you to do it."

Donald Ingram looked back and forth at his two companions and asked, "What's this about a hidden mine? I don't think I've heard about it."

"Oh, it was a big operation," replied Towner. "A gang of outlaws took over a gold mine in a mountain canyon that was so well hidden, it was almost impossible to find. Men traveling through these parts started vanishing into thin air; then pretty soon local men began disappearing. Finally a whole trainload of men who'd been hired by the railroad in Wichita to work at laying track between Denver and Cheyenne disappeared. Turned out they were being kidnapped and taken to the mine for slave labor. The outlaws worked them so hard, they were dying like flies."

Richard spoke up. "A vice-president of the Denver and Rio Grande Railroad was working with the outlaws, supplying the slaves. He's now behind bars at Canon City."

"We learned that a vicious tyrant named Raven was heading up the gang," Towner went on, "helped by a man named Clete Hobbs. They were getting filthy rich on the operation." Towner paused, glanced at Farrell, then looked back at Ingram and said, "Turned out that this Raven was a woman—a very beautiful and very deadly woman."

Tug Farrell lowered his head and rubbed the back of his neck. Ingram noticed it and asked, "Something touchy here, Tug?"

Farrell nodded, then replied in a tight voice, "You might say that. The woman in question had appeared in Denver one day, seemingly a lady in distress, calling herself Sheila Nevar. N-e-v-a-r. That's 'Raven' spelled backward. Anyway, I helped her out, and we quickly became friends." He paused. "Actually, the truth is I fell head over heels in love with her. I even went so far as to ask her to marry me. She put on a show like she was in love with me, too, using our relationship to keep me off guard about her clandestine operation. She told me she was the daughter of a rancher, and when I rode out toward the supposed ranch, following a map she had drawn, I was led into a trap. Seems Raven had decided I was getting too close to finding the mine for comfort, so she and her right-hand man, Hobbs, were going to kill me and dump my body in a mine shaft."

Shaking his head, Ingram observed, "She must have been some coldhearted female."

"Coldhearted *and* cold-blooded," replied Farrell bitterly.

"So what happened?" asked Ingram.

"I fortunately had some unexpected help show up in the form of the Ute Indians. While most of Raven's gang were fighting the Indians, I was battling Raven and a few of her cohorts in a big cabin that was built into the side of a mountain."

"Tell him about the shack above the canyon, Tug," cut in Webster Richards.

Farrell nodded. "Right. Well, before I was trapped, I found a small shack high above the canyon that had a trapdoor in its floor. It turned out to be a shaft that led down into the mine—a secret escape shaft that led down into a tunnel that came out in the back of the cabin. Raven and Hobbs had previously excavated the shaft in case they ever needed to escape in a hurry. At any rate, I could hear the sounds of men working far below. Not yet knowing that Sheila Nevar was actually the wicked Raven, I thought she had been captured and taken prisoner by Raven. To keep anyone from escaping from the shaft, I maneuvered large boulders weighing several hundreds of pounds on the lid of the trapdoor."

"Aha!" Ingram exclaimed, chuckling. "So I take it she and Hobbs tried to escape through that shaft!"

"Yeah," confirmed Farrell. "They managed to slip away from me into the tunnel. But before they could make good their escape, there was an explosion in the tunnel. The mountain caved in, sealing the shaft. If they were still alive after the explosion—which was doubtful —they had no way out."

"You said the boulders were still in place after the explosion?" queried Ingram.

"Yep."

"So if they survived the explosion, they died of suffocation."

Farrell nodded. "Unless somehow there was another source of air. If that was the case, they died of either dehydration or starvation. Tell you the truth, I never even checked the shaft, since I figured that much of an explosion had to have killed them. But one way or another, they died."

They were all silent for a long moment, and Tug Farrell's mind went to the article he had read that morning in the newspaper. Like a ghost dredged up from a sealed grave, the thought haunted him: *Would such a remarkable coincidence be possible?*

Breaking into the sheriff's reverie, Towner suggested, "Well, I hope you'll give our offer serious thought. We need you."

"Just can't do it, Clyde," replied the big man, shaking his head.

Towner studied him a few seconds, then asked, "You ever hear of Vic Devlin?"

"Sure," answered Farrell without hesitation. "He and his gang of bank robbers have been terrorizing towns all over Missouri, Oklahoma, and Kansas—and nearly every time they rob a bank, people get killed."

Nodding, Towner said, "That's right. And it looks like he's headed for Colorado."

Farrell stiffened. "What makes you think so?"

"One of our federal marshals had been trailing them across Kansas. They ambushed him and killed him just this side of Colby, which is less than sixty miles from the Colorado-Kansas border. We've alerted local lawmen by wire that Devlin and his blood-hungry bunch are in the area, moving west."

"There's another reason why we need you as a U.S. marshal, Tug," put in Richards. "Devlin is one mean and merciless cuss, and he's just cut us down by one."

"We need a man of your caliber to stop him," remarked Towner. "I have no doubt you can do it."

Farrell shook his head. "Like I said, gentlemen, I considered the idea of wearing a federal badge at one time, but I really can't do it now."

"Well, why not?" Towner queried.

Farrell sighed. "Because of my dad. He just came to live with me a few months ago, and I'm the only family he's got left. He's getting on, and he needs somebody around. If I took a U.S. marshal's appointment, I'd be traveling all the time. There'd be no one to look after the old fella. I just can't leave him. It wouldn't be right."

Disappointment showed on all three of the federal agents' faces. Towner sighed, saying, "Okay, Tug. I understand, and I can't fault you for seeing after your father."

The sheriff suddenly grinned. "I'll promise you this much: If Devlin shows up in my county, he'll live to regret it."

# Chapter Three

Vic Devlin and his bloody gang reined in under a stand of cottonwoods atop a hill a mile away from Goodland and gazed at the west-Kansas town. All eight riders had scraggly beards, greasy hair, sweat-stained hats, and filthy clothes—and they were all as unsavory as their appearance trumpeted.

Devlin himself—a thick-bodied, ugly man with a permanent sneer on his face and a mean look in his black eyes—was a venomous presence astride his horse. Scratching at his three-day growth of beard, the outlaw leader pulled a stolen watch from his pants pocket and glanced at the time. "Five after ten, boys," he grunted. "Bank's open now, so we might just as well go make our withdrawal."

Hoarse laughter made a round among the outlaws. Then Les Bean, who was second in command, asked, "Who do you want on guard outside the bank, Vic?"

Devlin's dark eyes assessed the faces arrayed in front of him before he announced, "Let's have Mel and Frank outside on this one."

Mel Stuart and Frank Waters nodded their agreement.

Each of the eight men pulled his gun, broke it open, and checked the loads. Returning the weapons to their holsters, the men nudged their mounts, then put them into a trot and headed for Goodland.

\* \* \*

Telegrapher Wally Loomis looked up from his desk
and glanced through the dusty, flyspecked window of
the telegraph office just as the eight riders made their
sudden appearance. As they headed slowly up the
town's main street, Loomis lifted his thin, frail body
from his chair and stepped close to the window. Peering
out, he suddenly swallowed hard, telling himself aloud,
"That's them, sure as shootin'!"

Loomis waited until the riders were a few yards
farther down the street, then opened the office door
and dashed along the boardwalk to the marshal's office.
Pushing the door open, he darted inside to find that
Marshal Hal Walsh was not there. He made a quick
inspection of the jail, then hurried back to the street
and looked up the block. The eight riders were almost
to the town's only bank.

The telegrapher crossed the street to the tobacco
shop and stuck his head in the doorway, asking the
proprietor, "Ralph, you seen the marshal?"

Receiving a negative reply, Loomis then ran to the
general store and hurried inside. Again getting no help,
seconds later he returned to the boardwalk and scurried up the street. The telegrapher then encountered
two elderly townsmen and asked them excitedly, "Has
either of you seen Marshal Walsh?"

One of them replied, "I saw him go into Curly
Beemer's place a little while ago."

"Thanks," Loomis called over his shoulder, already
hurrying toward the barber's shop. Nearing the shop,
he noted that six horses were tied at the hitch rail in
front of the Goodland State Bank, being watched over
by two of the gang members. Still in their saddles, the
twosome sat with their hands resting on the butts of
their holstered revolvers, looking up and down the
street in a suspicious manner.

Wally Loomis plunged through the doorway of
Curly Beemer's barbershop. A customer was reclining
in the chair with a hot towel wrapped around his head,

covering his face. The white apron over the man's upper body made it impossible to tell who it was.

When Beemer turned and looked at the telegrapher, the wiry little man gestured at the customer and asked, "Is that the marshal?"

The towel came off as Marshal Hal Walsh sat up quickly and answered himself, "Yes, it's me. Is something the matter, Wally?"

Loomis nodded forcefully. "Marshal, you remember that wire that came from the federal office in Kansas City a couple days ago? The one about Vic Devlin and his gang?"

"Of course," Walsh replied.

"Well, eight riders just rode in from the east side of town. They're at the bank this minute. Six are inside, and two are on their horses outside."

The marshal's face lost color. Throwing off the apron, he grabbed his hat from a wall peg, dropped it on his head, then whipped out his revolver. While checking the loads, he told the barber in a tight voice, "Curly, grab your shotgun. I'll see if I can get some more help." Snapping the cylinder of his Colt in place, the lawman opened the door cautiously and peered up the street. Curly Beemer came up behind him, cocking both hammers of his double-barreled twelve-gauge.

Suddenly gunfire was heard from inside the bank. Almost immediately after, six rough-looking men came charging out the door, two of them with guns smoking, and each man was carrying two cloth bags that were obviously stuffed full.

"No time to gather any more troops, Curly," shouted Walsh. "Come on! We've got to stop them!"

Wally Loomis said, "I'll help, Marshal, if there's a gun I can use."

The barber ran to a cabinet behind the barber chair and pulled open a drawer, producing a Colt .45. He made sure it was loaded, then snapped the cylinder shut and handed it to the little telegrapher. The marshal and the barber then darted out the doorway. Loomis thumbed back the hammer, swallowed nervously, and plunged outside behind them.

As Vic Devlin and his men settled into their saddles, one of his lookouts glanced down the street and saw the marshal coming on the run. Pointing toward Hal Walsh, the gang member shouted, "The law, boss!"

At the same instant, Marshal Walsh raised his gun, aiming it at the robbers, and commanded, "Hold it right there! You're all under arrest!"

Devlin instantly swung his revolver at the lawman and fired. At the same time, the rest of his men cut loose with their guns, and Walsh went down in a hail of hot lead. More bullets cut the air, ripping into the barber and the telegrapher, who were immediately behind the marshal.

Curly Beemer's shotgun boomed as he fell dead, sending a charge into a wagon that was parked along the side of the street. Wally Loomis gallantly rose up on his knees with blood pumping from two bullet wounds in his chest and brought the Colt to bear. Swearing at the man's tenacity, Vic Devlin put a bullet through his head. The frail body of the telegrapher flopped hard onto the ground and lay still.

Devlin turned toward his cohorts. "Let's go, men!" he shouted, and while the terrified townspeople looked on, the eight outlaws galloped out of Goodland, heading west.

An hour later the Devlin gang crossed the Colorado-Kansas border with their horses at a walk. Looking back over his shoulder, Armand Fix declared, "Ain't no posse gonna come, boss. That guy in the bank recognized you, and when he tells the rest of the town it was the Vic Devlin gang who robbed 'em, they'll be too scared to ride after us."

Ernie Osgood laughed and said, "That's the way we want to keep 'em—scared!"

Howard Smythe then asked, "How far's the next town, boss?"

"About twelve miles," replied Devlin. "Burlington."

"They got a bank?"

"Yep."

"We gonna clean it out?"

"Does the sun come up in the east?"

The gang members roared with laughter. Then Herb Frederick suggested, "How about we eat lunch when we first get to town, boss? All these towns have cafés."

"Good idea," Devlin agreed, chuckling, "seein' as how we'll be kinda busy afterwards."

They rode in silence for a while, and then Les Bean turned toward Devlin, reminding him, "You mentioned a day or two ago that you had big plans for Denver, Vic. Want to tell us about them now?"

"Sure," Devlin agreed while lighting a cigarette. He blew out a puff of smoke, then explained, "See, Denver's growin' in population. It's become a rail hub, and there's lots of cattle bein' raised around there. It's got *two* banks now, and I'm sure they're both filled with plenty of cash . . . and we're gonna hit 'em both at exactly the same time." The gang leader waited for the excited chatter of his men to die down, then added, "We'll have enough to get us to California with our pockets bulgin'."

Les Bean spoke up. "There's one thing that concerns me about this job, Vic."

Devlin blew out a smoke ring before remarking, "I'll bet I know what it is—or I guess I should say *who* it is: Tug Farrell."

"You hit the nail square on the head. The man's plenty tough, and he'll have to be reckoned with."

"I'm aware of that," Devlin answered calmly. "I've got a plan that'll take him out of the action." He looked at each man's expectant face and smiled. "See, we'll find us a small ranch not too far from Denver—one where there's just the rancher and his family, no hired hands to have to deal with. We'll take over the place and send the rancher into town to tell Farrell his family's bein' held hostage by a band of men. We won't give no names, 'cause if Farrell hears it's us, he'll know we're thinkin' of bank robbery."

Filling his lungs with smoke and letting it out slowly, Devlin continued, "The rancher'll tell Farrell the leader wants to talk to him, and if he don't come back immediately with the rancher, the man's family will be slaughtered."

Les Bean laughed. "Hey, that's smart thinkin', Vic. There's no way the sheriff can refuse to come. And I take it we won't be waitin' around for Farrell to show up."

"Right. Once the rancher rides off to take the message to Farrell, me and six of you men'll head for Denver. One of you will remain with the rancher's family to make sure they stay right there in the house. When that man sees the rancher returnin' with the sheriff, he can dash out the far side of the house, hop on his horse, and ride away, unseen. He'll circle around the rancher and the sheriff and head for Denver so he can meet the rest of us as we ride north out of town."

Bean scratched his head. "Why not just tie up the family? Why does one of us have to stay with them?"

"'Cause if somethin' goes wrong, we'll be able to use them for insurance."

"Sounds good so far, boss," commented Armand Fix. "How we gonna work takin' both banks at once?"

"Simple," replied the husky outlaw leader. "Four of you will enter the Rocky Mountain Bank at exactly the same time me and two others go into the Denver Community Bank. According to the article I read in the Denver newspaper, both banks are on the main street, and they're only a block apart. We'll clean 'em out and ride hard for Cheyenne, where we'll catch the next train west. By the time Tug Farrell gets back to town, we'll be long gone—and my days of outlawin' will be over."

Herb Frederick shook his head in disbelief. "Boss, are you sure after all these years you'll be able to quit the outlaw trail? Are you sure you won't get bored runnin' a saloon and casino?"

Vic Devlin chuckled. "Are you kiddin'? I can't wait to get to San Francisco. With what's in my saddlebags at the moment and what I'm gonna add in Denver, I'll be sittin' pretty. Like I promised you boys before, you'll each have a job in my place and share in the profits. We'll live like kings for the rest of our lives—and have plenty of ladies-in-waiting to serve us!"

As Sheriff Tug Farrell trudged wearily toward home, his thoughts were of the Harrison family—especially Clara. He had decided it was better that he not pay his condolences, feeling that seeing him would only make things harder for the poor woman. Sighing deeply, he lifted his gaze to the magnificent jagged peaks of the Rockies, a sight that usually invigorated him. But this time it merely served to thrust his mind back to the newspaper article he had read earlier, and he knew he would have to resolve the constantly nagging doubt he now had about the fate of Raven Morrow and Clete Hobbs.

Farrell reached his house, and when he shoved open the door, he took a deep whiff of the aroma wafting from the kitchen. Hanging his hat on a peg in the hallway, Farrell hurried to the kitchen, where he found his father stirring a stew at the big wood-burning stove.

Maynard Farrell's wrinkled face broke into a smile at the sight of his son. "Howdy, Tug," he said, brushing back a lock of silver hair that had fallen over his eyes. "Thought you might like some good cookin' for a change. I'm surprised that stuff you concoct hasn't killed you by now, seein' as how you eat it all the time."

The sheriff laughed as he crossed to the sink and started working the pump handle, filling a basin. As Farrell washed up, his father dished out bowls of the steaming food and put them on the table. They sat down, and the lawman immediately grabbed his fork and shoved it into the bowl. But his hand froze halfway to his mouth when Maynard loudly cleared his throat.

He met his father's gaze, and the old man said with a grin, "Still forgit, don'tcha?"

The younger Farrell dropped his fork and bowed his head while his father said grace. He murmured "Amen" after Maynard did, then began eating with gusto.

While they ate, Maynard talked expansively about the events of the day. Periodically, the old gent paused in his speech, waiting for his son's comments, but none came. When they were almost finished eating, Maynard cocked his head, squinted at his offspring, and declared, "You're a talkative cuss, ain'tcha?"

Looking across at his father, Farrell asked, "What's that?"

"I said you're sure a talkative cuss tonight. Have you heard anything I've said?"

"Oh, uh . . . sure, Pop. Sure."

The senior Farrell laid down his fork, pushed his bowl away, and demanded, "Okay, out with it. What's disturbin' you?"

Farrell grinned slowly. "What makes you think something's disturbing me?"

"Hey, kid, this is your ol' pappy talkin'," reminded the oldster. "If I recollect right, I've known you for about thirty-seven years. I can tell when somethin's disturbin' my boy. Come on. Let's hear it. You in love again?"

Farrell chuckled, shaking his head. "No, Pop, I'm not in love again. I've just got something on my mind."

"Bothered about havin' to blow them Harrison brothers to judgment, are ya?"

"I'm not happy about having had to kill them, Pop, but what's bothering me is something I read in the *Sentinel* this morning." He shoved back his chair and stood up. "While we clean up the kitchen, I'll tell you about it."

As the two men did the dishes, Tug Farrell related the story of the slave mine, then told the old man about the article in the newspaper. Their kitchen duty finished, they went into the parlor, lit a couple of lamps, and sat down on the horsehair sofa. "So you see, Pop," the lawman concluded, "it seems like too much of a coincidence that there could be two such couples running two identical operations."

Maynard stroked his chin thoughtfully, then said, "I'll have to agree with you, son. Sounds like maybe that Raven woman and her cohort lived through the explosion and found a way outta the mine."

Sighing, Farrell stated, "Yeah, and my curiosity's getting the better of me. I've simply got to know for sure if that couple in the Sacramento County jail are actually Raven Morrow and Clete Hobbs. Besides, if they are, they need to be brought back here to face murder charges."

"So what are you gonna do? Go out to California?"

Farrell shook his head. "Not just yet. First things first. I'm going to ride out to the mine tomorrow morning and take a look under the trapdoor in that old shack and see if I can find out anything."

The early-October air was crisp as Deputy Harlon Stang made his way along the boardwalk shortly before eight o'clock the following morning. He would show his boss that he could be early to work. Drawing near the sheriff's office, Stang was surprised to see Maynard Farrell standing in front of the door, apparently waiting for him.

Maynard smiled as he said, " 'Mornin', Harlon. Tug asked me to meet you here and let you know that he's gonna be outta town till sometime this afternoon."

"How come?" asked Stang.

"Come on inside and I'll tell you," replied the old man. "Tug said you weren't here three years ago, so you'd need some information to understand where he's gone and why."

Sheriff Tug Farrell had ridden out of Denver at dawn, heading into the mountains. By the time he skirted the rim of the dark canyon, the sun was midway through the morning sky—although the area was so densely timbered that the sunlight barely penetrated to the forest floor. Memories flooded his mind, and he remembered as clearly as if it were yesterday the day he had ridden to the canyon to rescue Sheila Nevar from abductors, only to find that he had been led into a trap. He wondered how he could have been so blind as to fall in love with such a crafty, cunning woman, then reminded himself it was partly because she was so stunningly beautiful. He was first mesmerized by her beauty, and then she captured his heart by pretending to be sweet, kind, and considerate.

Farrell shook his head as if to throw the bitter memories from his mind. Then he spurred his horse toward the clearing in which there stood an old barn and several small shacks, including the one that contained the trapdoor that covered the escape shaft.

Dismounting, the big lawman looked around thoroughly. It appeared that no one had been there since the day the mine had been closed down. He removed the lantern and coil of rope he had attached to the saddle horn, then walked to the shack. Pulling open the creaky door, he stepped inside.

The boulders still rested on the trapdoor, just where he had left them. He then did the reverse of what he had done three years earlier: Looping the rope around the boulders, he tied the other end to the pommel and used his horse's strength to work them off the lid. With his heart pounding, Tug Farrell lit the lantern and pulled open the trapdoor, then peered into the dark abyss. As far down as he could see, the ladder was intact.

Farrell hooked the lantern onto his belt loop, then began a slow descent into the shaft. After climbing down some forty feet, he made out rocks and dirt in a heap at the bottom—the result of the explosion. Continuing his careful descent down the ladder, he replayed in his mind what must have happened that fateful day: While he was busy fighting Raven's henchmen in the cabin, she and Hobbs had darted into the mine. They undoubtedly had climbed up the escape

shaft and probably had time to reach the top before the
dynamite exploded.

The lawman tried to reconstruct what happened
next: Had they reached the trapdoor, been unable to
get out, then climbed back down into the tunnel and
died in the explosion? He did not see any skeletons to
confirm it. Did that mean their bodies were buried beneath the rubble? He hardly thought so. He doubted
they would have had time to climb all the way up and
then all the way down again before the dynamite went
off. They must have been somewhere on the ladder
when the explosion occurred. But then where were
their remains?

Another half-minute brought him to the bottom,
and he stood on top of the tons of rubble, peering into
the gloom. No, they could not have gotten out by the
direction they had come, for the tunnel back to the
cabin was completely blocked. He turned around, and
suddenly something caught his eye. There seemed to be
a source of light. Quickly he doused the lantern, and he
realized that a weak shaft of light was filtering from the
back side of the pile of rubble. Scurrying over the rubble, Farrell saw that the source was an opening at the
top of a long, angled shaft that obviously topped out
somewhere on the mountain. It was easily large enough
for a man—and a woman—to crawl through. Apparently the explosion had opened a weak spot, creating a
natural shaft.

There was no question now in the lawman's mind:
The couple in the Sacramento County jail calling themselves Rita Marston and Clarence Hoffman were Raven
Morrow and Clete Hobbs. The two bloody murderers
had survived the explosion and escaped, and were now
awaiting trial for running a slave camp in the Sierras.
Recollecting the article, Farrell realized there had been
nothing said about any of the slaves having died. That
meant that the sentence would be comparatively light.
The lawman needed to get them extradited to Colorado
so they could be tried for multiple murders and hang
for their crimes.

Stunned by the impact of learning that the nefarious pair was still alive, Sheriff Tug Farrell climbed the ladder back to the surface. He waited a few minutes for his eyes to readjust to the light, and then he mounted his horse and rode hard back to Denver.

It was late afternoon by the time Tug Farrell entered his office. The moment he did, both Harlon Stang and Maynard Farrell asked at the same time, "What did you find out at the mine?"

The sheriff let out a long sigh, then replied, "Just what I didn't want to." He hung his Stetson on a peg, then sank heavily into his chair and continued, "Apparently the explosion opened a passageway for them to get out. As sure as I'm sitting here, Raven Morrow and Clete Hobbs are alive and right this minute behind bars in the Sacramento County jail."

"What are you going to do?" Maynard asked.

"Well, I just wired the sheriff there, telling him who I believe his prisoners really are and that they're wanted here on murder charges. I also told him that I'm going to board the next train for Sacramento to identify the pair and asked him not to allow a trial to take place before I arrive. If my assumption is correct, I'll seek extradition so a federal marshal can bring them back to Denver to stand trial for murder." He rubbed his neck wearily. "I asked the sheriff for an immediate acknowledgment."

Just before sundown, a return wire came from Sheriff Bob Sovern stating that he would be expecting Farrell and that the pending trial had been postponed. Pleased with his fellow lawman's fast response, Farrell hurried to Denver's Union Station to buy a ticket for Sacramento. The Denver Pacific train would leave for Cheyenne three days later, at six A.M. on Friday, and the connecting Union Pacific train bound for Sacramento would leave at noon on the same day.

Over supper that evening, Tug and Maynard Farrell discussed the lawman's pending trip. After a while, the conversation turned to old times and the happiness they had had in the days when Farrell was growing up. Leaving the kitchen, they walked to the parlor, and Tug Farrell suddenly turned and hugged his father. "Pop, I'm sorry that Sarah had to catch the fever and die, but I sure am glad to have you here with me."

Maynard patted his son's back while returning the hug, and in a slightly choked voice murmured, "And I'm mighty glad to be here. If the good Lord's willin', we'll have a lot of happy times together in the days to come."

# Chapter Four

The small farm with the stream snaking across it, bisecting the spread, looked serene in the October morning sun. The single-level white house huddled beneath a stand of cottonwood trees—brilliant with red, orange, and yellow leaves—while across the yard sat the outbuildings. Thin tendrils of smoke from the chimney at the rear of the house lifted lazily into the clear Colorado sky. Visible across four or five miles of tawny prairie grass was Denver, while looming like a backdrop behind the fast-growing town were the towering Rocky Mountains, their high peaks already snowcapped.

Sitting their horses on a small mound above the farm, Vic Devlin and his henchmen were oblivious of the beauty of the scene. They were focusing on two figures pitching hay onto a wagon from a loaf-shaped haystack in a field about a hundred yards from the ranch buildings.

Devlin flipped his cigarette to the ground, then said, "Looks like the perfect setup, boys. Just what we were lookin' for. There's no bunkhouse, no house for a hired hand, so it's gotta be a family operation."

Les Bean remarked, "I think one of those two out there at the haystack is a kid. Probably the rancher's son."

"Which one of us stays with the family, boss?" asked Herb Frederick.

Devlin regarded the man with his cold black eyes and asked, "You volunteerin'?"

Frederick shrugged his shoulders. "Sure, if that's the way you want it. Let's get to it."

"Not yet," said Devlin. "I want the rancher and the kid close to the house when we move in." He grinned. "You gotta learn more patience, Herb. Them banks ain't goin' nowhere."

Rancher Paul Warren and his sixteen-year-old son slid off the haystack, pitchforks in hand, onto the wagon. The lanky Warren stabbed his pitchfork into the load of hay and climbed onto the wagon seat. The towheaded youth, virtually a carbon copy of his father, did likewise, then said, "I think we should keep loadin' awhile longer, Pa."

Laughing, Warren responded, "I'm two and a half times your age, son, and I don't have the kind of energy you do. Let's get this stuff inside."

Danny clucked to the team, snapping the reins, and the heavily loaded wagon started rolling toward the barn, scattering squawking chickens out of the way. They had gone about fifty yards when the youth pointed across the prairie to the east. "Pa, look. Riders. 'Pears like they're headed our way."

Warren squinted into the sun, shading his eyes. After a moment he declared, "I don't like the looks of them. I'd say they were no-account drifters."

"I wonder what they want with us," Danny murmured.

"I don't know, but we'll soon find out. They're turning in here, all right."

The eight shabby-looking riders drew rein in the yard at the rear of the house. The riders dismounted at the same moment that Opal Warren appeared on the back porch with flour on her hands and a dish towel draped over one shoulder. Tall and slender like her husband and about the same age, the blond-haired woman was rather plain in a fresh-scrubbed way.

Opal flicked a glance at the hay wagon as it drew near the barn, then swept her eyes over the scraggly faces of the eight men and asked, "Is there something I can do for you gentlemen?"

Ignoring her question, Vic Devlin queried, "That your husband and kid comin' in on that wagon?"

"Yes," answered Opal, defensively taking a step backward on the porch.

"You got any more kids in the house?" asked Les Bean.

The apprehension that had been in the woman's pale blue eyes turned to fear. "What business is it of yours?" she demanded, her voice brittle.

Devlin raised a hand, motioning for Bean to be quiet. Turning in the direction of the wagon as the rancher and his son drew closer, the outlaw leader took a few steps in their direction and smiled. "Howdy. What's your name, rancher?"

Paul Warren regarded the thick-bodied, ugly man with grim-faced suspicion. His tone was not friendly as he responded, "Who wants to know?"

Devlin was clearly angered by the curt reply. Before he could voice it, however, Les Bean stared at the rancher and growled, "My friend asked you a civil question, mister! Now, you give him a civil answer!"

The rancher put his hands on his hips and retorted caustically, "You're on *my* property, mister. I'll ask the questions here."

Suddenly Les Bean whipped out his gun, and the others, except for Devlin, followed suit. Opal screamed, and her son, standing next to his father, looked to see what the rancher would do.

Paul Warren's body went rigid. Glaring at the leader, he demanded of Devlin, "What do you want?"

"The first thing I want," replied Devlin coolly, "is an answer to my question. What's your name?"

"Paul Warren," came the quick response.

"Anybody else on the place?"

Warren did not answer. Devlin turned around and said, "Mel, Ernie, check the house."

The two men headed for the back porch and Warren suddenly dashed after them. Les Bean fired his gun, putting a bullet in the dirt directly in front of the rancher. Warren stopped short and looked at him. "You stay right there, Mr. Warren," Bean warned.

Danny Warren hurried to his terrified mother and put an arm around her shoulder. The two outlaws disappeared through the doorway, and almost instantly a scream was heard. Opal began to whimper, and her husband glared at Bean and rasped, "They'd better not harm her."

Bean merely grinned wickedly. " 'Her,' is it?"

Presently the two men emerged from the house, each holding the arm of a fourteen-year-old girl. "Daddy!" she cried. "What are they going to do to us?"

"Nothing, Darlene," assured Warren, obviously trying to sound convincing but not succeeding. Then, turning to Devlin, he commanded, "Tell them to let go of her!"

The outlaw leader threw his head back and laughed. "Hey, rancher," he roared, "you act like you're holdin' guns on us, not the other way 'round!"

Ignoring Devlin and the weapon in Les Bean's hand, Warren walked over to the two outlaws holding his daughter and blocked them from moving any farther. His fury was evident as he commanded, "Let go of her!"

Vic Devlin stepped beside the rancher and told his men, "It's all right, boys. Do as the man says."

Darlene Warren, who was a younger stamp of her mother, dashed into her father's arms. Warren again demanded of Devlin, "What do you want with us?"

"Let's go in the house and I'll tell you," replied Devlin calmly.

Moments later, the Warren family and the Devlin gang were clustered in the kitchen, with the Warrens seated at the table. Surrounding them with their guns still drawn, the gang members were a menacing presence as Devlin looked the rancher in the eye and said, "You're gonna run a little errand for us, Mr. Warren."

"Errand?" echoed the rancher, his tone obstinate. Without a word, Devlin drew his revolver, thumbed back the hammer, and pointed it at Opal's head. The woman gasped and eyed her husband pleadingly.

Through his teeth Devlin snarled, "I don't like your attitude, Warren. Now, I suggest you change it, 'cause if you don't, there's gonna be some blood shed around here—starting with your wife's. You understand?"

Warren's face went chalky. "All right, all right. I'll run your errand for you. Just put your gun away."

Devlin grinned triumphantly, eased the hammer into place, and holstered the gun. "I'm glad to see we understand each other. Okay, let's get down to business. I assume you're acquainted with your county sheriff."

"I know Tug Farrell, yes."

"Good. I want you to saddle up your horse and ride into town. Find Farrell and tell him he's got to ride back to the ranch with you immediately—and I do mean immediately. You tell him if we don't see the two of you ridin' hard this way within the next half hour, your wife and these kids are dead. Got it?"

"What do you want with Farrell?" queried Warren.

"That ain't none of your business, mister!" bellowed Les Bean. "You just do what you're told! Now, git!"

Paul Warren looked at his terrified family. Rising to his feet, the rancher said, "I'll have Farrell back here as soon as I can. But I want your promise that my wife and children will not be harmed in any way."

Scowling, Devlin rasped, "You want a promise? Okay, I promise you they'll all die unless you're back here with that sheriff in thirty minutes!"

"You can't be so stringent on this!" argued Warren. "What if Farrell's out of town, or something like that? You can't—"

"You're wastin' time!" bellowed Devlin.

Paul Warren flicked a reassuring glance at his family, then dashed outside. Moments later he was on his horse and galloping past the house, and soon the sound of rapid hoofbeats faded and was gone.

Devlin waited for a few minutes, then signaled his men that it was time to leave. Opal Warren and her two children looked on in puzzlement as seven of the outlaws hurried out and mounted up, then galloped out of the yard, heading west. Only Herb Frederick remained behind, and he sat down at the table, gun in hand, taking the chair Paul Warren had occupied.

Opal Warren stared intently at Frederick for a long moment, then asked, "What is going on? Are you supposed to kill us, now that my husband's gone?"

"Naw, I ain't gonna kill you, lady," Frederick answered. "Tell ya what, I'll let you in on our plans, seein' as how you can't do nothin' about it. But you know what? I'd like some coffee first. You got some, don't you?"

"Of course," Opal replied quickly and cordially, anxious to stay on Frederick's good side. Pushing her chair back, she added, "The stove's already hot. I'll make you some in a jiffy."

"Sit still, Mom," Danny suddenly spoke up, rising. "I'll put the coffeepot on and stoke up the fire. You keep Darlene company."

Opal nodded and reached for her daughter's hand under the table. The outlaw watched as Danny first added wood to the fire, then pumped water into the coffeepot. Noting the wads of dough on the counter by the sink, Frederick said to Opal, "Looks like you're bakin' bread."

"I was—until you and your bunch rode in here."

"My mother was a great baker," remarked Frederick, ignoring the woman's caustic tone.

Opal gave him a hard glare, then asked, "I wonder what your mother would say if she could see you sitting there holding a gun on me."

The outlaw's face stiffened. "She's dead, lady," he said flatly. When the rancher's wife murmured that she was sorry, Frederick's demeanor softened. "So, you was wantin' to know what's goin' on. Okay, I'll tell you. My pals are plannin' a bank robbery, and sendin' your husband for the sheriff is a trick to get Farrell out of town so's he can't interfere." He sniffed, adding, "If they're smart, nobody else will interfere either. My boss, he don't cotton to no interferin'. People who try usually end up dead."

Opal Warren's heart sank. The family's life savings were in the Denver Community Bank, and she wondered if that was the bank they were planning on robbing. Then she silently admonished herself for worrying about money when people's lives might be at stake. She gave her children a hopeless look, knowing there was nothing they could do to stop the robbery. But Danny, now standing by the stove behind the outlaw, looked furtively at his mother, silently indicating that she should try to divert Frederick's attention.

Half-fearful for what her son was planning but knowing they had to do something, Opal Warren began chatting garrulously. "Where were you raised, Mr. . . . ? Oh. I don't know your name, but I suppose that's deliberate, isn't it? Anyway, where were you brought up? I hope you don't mind my asking, but since we're all stuck here together for a while, we may as well get to know each other."

Obviously glad that the family was being so compliant, Herb Frederick relaxed and leaned back in his chair, then began recounting his life story. Directly behind him, Danny Warren wiped his sweaty hands on his pants and cautiously, quietly picked up the heavy skillet sitting on the stove. Her heart pounding, Opal had to force herself to keep her eyes off her son and firmly focused on the unsuspecting outlaw.

Frederick was in the middle of a sentence when Danny turned slowly around and, the improvised club raised high, brought the skillet down hard on the outlaw's head. The outlaw first slumped over the table, and then he slowly slid from his chair and tumbled to the floor.

Opal and her son dragged the unconscious Frederick outside and across the yard while Darlene ran to the barn for some rope. They laid him under the end of the hay wagon, then tied his feet to one wheel and his hands to the one on the opposite side. As soon as the outlaw was secured, Danny jumped on Frederick's already saddled horse—saving precious minutes—and galloped toward town to warn Sheriff Tug Farrell of what was about to take place.

Danny had ridden just over two miles when he met up with the sheriff and his father. Reining in, he breathlessly told the two men how he had clobbered Herb Frederick and about the bank robbery that was going to take place.

Tug Farrell asked immediately, "Did they say which bank they're going to rob, Danny?"

"No, sir," replied the youth, shaking his head. "All the outlaw said was that his pals were planning a bank robbery in Denver, and we were held hostage as a means to get you out of town so you couldn't interfere."

The lawman hurriedly told Paul Warren, "From the description you gave me of the gang leader, I was almost certain it was Vic Devlin. Now that I know a bank robbery's in the making, I've no doubt it's him. You and Danny go on back to the ranch and keep an eye on Devlin's crony." With that, Farrell wheeled his horse around and spurred it back toward town.

Maynard Farrell entered the Denver Community Bank at ten-forty-five that morning to draw some money from his account. He was one of five customers in the bank at that moment. A middle-aged man was seated beside the bank president's desk over in a far corner, while two women and a man were standing at a counter making out deposit slips.

The oldster approached the window and greeted the teller, a small bald-headed man. " 'Mornin', Cecil. I need to get ten dollars from you."

Moments later, the old man turned away from the window, stuffing several bills into his wallet, and smiled at the woman now waiting her turn. As Maynard walked toward the door, two young cowhands entered the bank, and the senior Farrell recognized Jerry Hill and Martin Findlay from the Diamond T ranch a few miles south of Denver. Tug Farrell and the ranch's owner were close friends, and when Maynard had visited the ranch with his son, he had become acquainted with Jerry and Martin.

Both cowboys smiled warmly when they saw the old man.

"Howdy, Mr. Farrell," chirped Jerry Hill.

"Good 'mornin', Mr. Farrell," said Martin Findlay. "You puttin' money in or takin' it out?"

"Howdy, boys," Maynard replied with a grin. "Takin' it out this time."

Maynard followed the ranch hands over to the counter, where they pulled out their paychecks to endorse them, dipping the bank's pens into inkwells.

They were chatting away when the door opened yet again. Jerry Hill happened to glance up as Vic Devlin, Mel Stuart, and Ernie Osgood filed in, and he flinched. Martin Findlay noticed the panic that leapt into the eyes of his friend and, cocking his head, he asked, "Jerry, what's the matter?"

"This place is about to be robbed," whispered Hill. "One of the guys who just came in is Vic Devlin. I recognize him from a wanted poster I saw over in Salina a few months ago." The outlaws had not yet drawn their guns, but were looking around, assessing the situation.

Maynard Farrell heard Martin's words. Moving close to Hill, he asked softly, "You know those three dudes?"

"I know the big ugly one," confirmed Hill, still speaking in a whisper. "He's bad. Real bad. Drop down next to the wall, Mr. Farrell. I've got to stop this!"

Even as he spoke, Jerry Hill drew his revolver and shouted, "Look out, everybody! Those three men are bank robbers!"

Ernie Osgood saw Hill go for his gun and whipped out his own weapon. Customers screamed and scattered, then Osgood fired, hitting Hill in the chest. More screams filled the bank, echoing off the high ceiling, and the other two outlaws brought up their guns. Martin Findlay fired at Ernie Osgood a split second after the outlaw shot Hill. The bullet missed Osgood by a hair-breadth and splintered a wall on the other side of the bank.

Customers and bank employees, including the bank president, flattened themselves on the floor. Swearing loudly, Mel Stuart fired at Findlay point-blank, putting the slug into his heart. The impact of the slug hitting his chest drove Martin Findlay backward, and he thudded into the counter, then collapsed on the floor.

Kneeling beside the crumpled form of Jerry Hill, Maynard Farrell looked at him with pity. The young man was still breathing, although with difficulty, and blood from his wound was spilling onto the wooden floor. It was obvious that he was dying.

Vic Devlin waved his gun menacingly and bellowed, "All right, everybody, if you don't want to die like those two, stay right where you are and keep your hands where we can see 'em!" To his cohorts he said, "Ernie, you go clean out the safe. Mel, get the money in the teller's cage."

Maynard Farrell looked up at the outlaw leader, who was barking orders while pacing about, gun in hand, then back at the cowboy. His jaw clenched, Maynard felt anger surging through him. Then he spotted the butt of Jerry's revolver protruding from under his body where it had dropped when he was hit.

The oldster surreptitiously looked back at Devlin, who was still pacing and shouting out warnings and orders. Maynard felt his throat go dry. Gritting his teeth, he reached down and palmed the revolver, then thumbed back the hammer. But as Maynard, slowed by age, brought the revolver to bear, Vic Devlin saw him. His vastly greater speed and experience giving him the edge, the outlaw leader grinned evilly as he quickly lined the muzzle of his gun between the old man's eyes and fired. Maynard Farrell's body slammed against the floor beside Jerry Hill's.

Pivoting around with the smoking gun in his hand, Devlin blared, "Anyone else in this place want to die?

Huh? Just try what the old geezer did, and I'll be glad to oblige!"

Mel Stuart came away from the teller's cage carrying a bag full of money, and Devlin commanded, "Give me that and go help Ernie at the safe. Make it snappy! We've got to get out of here!"

Inside the Rocky Mountain Bank one block north of the Community Bank, Les Bean and his three cohorts were painstakingly cleaning out the two tellers' cages and the bank's large vault while customers and employees stood with hands raised over their heads, eyes filled with fear. Standing behind his desk, his hands raised, a bank officer eyed the desk drawer near his right leg. Inside was a loaded .38-caliber revolver—and if he got the opportunity, he would use it.

Suddenly the sound of gunfire reverberated from down the street. The bank robbers shot quick glances at each other, and Armand Fix called, "Les, that's comin' from the direction of the other bank! Vic and the others must've run into some trouble!"

"Yeah," agreed Bean. "We better take what we've got in the bags and get outta here right now!"

As the four outlaws charged toward the door, the bank officer reached in his desk drawer, picked up the .38, and fired at them. Armand Fix was already outside when Howard Smythe took the bullet in his shoulder and went down. The money bag he was carrying slipped from his fingers, as did his revolver. The bank officer was cocking his gun, about to fire again, when Les Bean whirled around and fired twice, killing the man. Two female employees screamed with horror as the officer sprawled over his desk. Bean held his revolver menacingly on the small crowd as he grabbed the fallen money bag, then backed toward the door while Frank Waters helped Smythe to his horse.

Just as Bean was settling in his saddle, a bank customer appeared at the door wielding the fallen revolver. The man fired at Bean but missed. Cursing, the outlaw shot the customer through the head, then turned to Frank Waters. "If you don't get Smythe onto his horse immediately, we'll have to leave him here!" he warned.

Suddenly a lone rider came galloping down the street from the north, and the morning sun glinted off the badge on his chest. "Les!" shouted Armand Fix. "That's gotta be Farrell!"

Before Bean could respond, Tug Farrell skidded his horse to a stop thirty yards away and leapt from the saddle, gun blazing. Just as Waters planted Smythe in the saddle, one of Farrell's slugs tore into Smythe, killing him instantly. Smythe's body peeled out of the saddle as Waters, Fix, and Bean fired back at the lawman and dove for cover behind a stack of wooden crates in front of the general store next door to the bank. When Armand Fix rose from behind a crate to fire at the sheriff, Farrell's sixth bullet found its mark in his throat.

Jumping behind a wagon parked at the side of the street, Farrell quickly reloaded his gun. Seconds later he saw Frank Waters appear from behind the boxes, and he fired at Waters's head. The outlaw pulled back, but the bullet chewed the corner off the box, and it sent splinters flying into his face. Waters's howls gave the lawman satisfaction.

Swearing at Farrell, Les Bean exposed his head and shoulder long enough to fire two shots. A return slug from the sheriff's gun clipped the corner where Bean's head had been a split second before, then ricocheted away, keening wildly.

The two horses that were hitched to the wagon where Farrell had hunkered began to dance about nervously, snorting and tossing their heads. The lawman was looking around, considering a better vantage point, when Bean reappeared and sent three more shots at him.

Holding his fire for a more advantageous moment, Farrell wondered where Vic Devlin was. Paul Warren had told him there were eight outlaws in all, which meant Devlin had to be somewhere with two more men. Perhaps there had been a shoot-out inside the

bank. Were Devlin and the other two lying in there
with bullets in them?

Farrell knew he had to flush the two outlaws out
from behind the boxes. Thinking fast, he decided to use
the frightened team of horses to his advantage. The
animals were aimed straight for the crates, which were
stacked so that they protruded into the street. If the
team were sent into the boxes, the men would have to
come out.

Two more bullets sang past the sheriff's head as he
scurried to the front of the wagon and released the
brake. He then slapped the nearest horse hard on the
rump, and when the animal bolted, it took its partner
with it. Both horses charged ahead, directly toward the
stack of boxes. They veered at the last moment, but the
bounding wagon struck the crates and sent them scattering.

Down the street, Vic Devlin and his two partners
emerged from the Community Bank and looked in the
direction of the gunfire. As they dashed to their horses
they could see Howard Smythe and Armand Fix
sprawled on the ground, although they could not tell
how Les Bean and Frank Waters were faring.

Devlin told Mel Stuart and Ernie Osgood, "Let's
ride!"

"Wait a minute, Vic!" shouted Stuart. "We can't just
leave Les and Frank! Let's go help 'em!"

"Look, we don't know how many men they're
facin' or even if either of them's already dead!" retorted
Devlin. "We're liable to get caught or killed if we try to
help 'em!" As he spoke, he vaulted into his saddle, gripping two money bags in one hand.

Stuart and Osgood looked at each other. Finally,
shrugging their shoulders, they mounted up and
spurred their mounts after Devlin's.

As they headed away, the bank manager appeared
at the doorway with a gun in his hand. He opened fire,
and his bullet caught Osgood, who was bringing up the
rear. The outlaw screamed with pain and slumped over

in the saddle, but clinging to the saddle horn, he managed to follow his cohorts. They turned the corner and galloped to the next street, avoiding the gunfight going on in front of the Rocky Mountain Bank, then turned and headed out of town.

When they reached the north edge of town, where Herb Frederick was to have been waiting, Devlin signaled for Stuart and Osgood to stop. He looked around for Frederick, and when it became obvious that he was nowhere in the vicinity, Devlin declared, "Somethin' went haywire, but we can't wait. We'll have to go on without him." Then he turned to Ernie Osgood and asked coldly, "Can you ride?"

Osgood straightened slightly, still clutching the saddle horn. Blood bubbled through the shredded hole in his shirt. Breathing hard, he gasped, "I . . . I've got to."

"Okay," said their leader, "but if you start slowin' down, we'll have to leave you. We've got a train to catch in Cheyenne—and nothin' or no one's gonna keep me from it."

# Chapter Five

Sheriff Tug Farrell stood with his weapon aimed and cocked, ready to fire, as Les Bean and Frank Waters ran out from behind the scattered wooden boxes. Waters was still cursing the splinters in his face and eyes, but Bean spotted the lawman and raised his weapon.

"Drop the gun, mister!" the sheriff bellowed.

Les Bean ignored the warning, bringing the gun into play. Farrell squeezed the trigger, and the revolver roared and bucked against his palm.

Grunting from the impact of the slug that tore into his stomach, the outlaw gripped the wound with his left hand while his right fired the gun reflexively, sending the bullet into the street ten feet in front of Farrell. Bean staggered a few steps as blood began pouring around his hand. Then the revolver slipped from his fingers and he crumpled to the ground.

Moments later, Frank Waters, blinking wildly, brought his gun to bear on the lawman and fired. Farrell shot simultaneously, his aim true, and the slug exploded Waters's heart as the outlaw's bullet hummed harmlessly past Farrell.

Striding over to the two dead men, Farrell stared down at them. People began appearing at windows and in doorways, and harried voices could be heard from inside the bank.

"Sheriff!" a man called. "Sheriff, come quick!"

Farrell turned to see Cecil Marks, the Community Bank's teller, running toward him.

The little bald-headed man drew up, eyes bulging, and sucked hard for breath. Gasping, Marks said, "Sheriff, they robbed our bank, too! Apparently . . . apparently they hit us both . . . at the same time."

Farrell looked toward the Community Bank, realizing his occupation with the four robbers of the Rocky Mountain Bank had kept him from hearing the shooting up the street. Looking down at the teller as he broke open his gun to reload it, the sheriff remarked, "I suppose the robbers are gone by now."

"Yes, sir. Several people told me they saw them ride north out of town."

"How many were there?"

"Three of them, Sheriff."

"Anybody hurt?"

Cecil Marks licked his lips nervously. "Uh . . . yes, sir. Jerry Hill and Martin Findlay from the Diamond T tried to stop the robbers. Martin is dead, and Jerry is badly shot up. I don't think he'll make it."

Farrell shook his head despondently. "I'm real sorry to hear that. Has somebody gone for Doc?"

"Yes, sir," Marks assured him. "But . . . but, Sheriff, there was somebody else in the bank when the robbers came in. I mean, somebody else that got shot."

"Who was it?" asked Farrell, slipping his loaded revolver into its holster.

The little man scrubbed a nervous hand over his mouth. "Well, sir, it was your father."

Farrell blanched. "My father?" he echoed, his voice rising. "Pop was in the bank?"

"Yes."

"Did you say he got shot?"

"Yes, sir," came the reply. Obviously unable to meet the sheriff's questioning gaze, Marks looked down at his feet and mumbled, "Your . . . father is dead, Sheriff."

The lawman felt as if something had exploded inside his head. "Dead?" he asked as if disbelieving his ears. "My father's dead?"

Before the teller could respond, the lawman was

racing down the street toward the Community Bank. *No!* his mind screamed. *Please, God! It can't be! Don't let Pop be dead!*

A large crowd was gathered around the doorway of the bank as Tug Farrell reached the building. Elbowing his way through the press of onlookers, Farrell hurried inside. A glance revealed the body of Martin Findlay sprawled on the floor. Nearby, a cluster of people, including Dr. Fred Halsey, surrounded Jerry Hill. Another glance inside the circle of people revealed what his mind at first refused to see: the lifeless form of his father.

Farrell felt a wave of nausea wash over him. Removing his hat, he pushed his way through the bystanders and knelt beside Maynard Farrell's body. Then he saw the bullet hole between Maynard's eyes and his blood splattered on the wall behind him. Suddenly the lawman felt as if the room were spinning, and his stomach churned. Reaching for the elderly Farrell's cold hand, he mumbled, "Oh, Pop, how did this happen?"

Dr. Fred Halsey left Jerry Hill's side and went to the sheriff. He laid a consoling hand on Farrell's shoulder, saying softly, "I'm sorry, Tug. Truly sorry. He was a wonderful man."

Almost overcome with grief, yet filled with wrath at the same time, Tug Farrell stood up and looked around at everyone inside the bank, asking, "Did anybody see how this happened?"

The bank president drew close and replied, "We were all on the floor, Sheriff. I don't think any of us saw it."

"I did," Jerry Hill hoarsely whispered.

Farrell went over to him, kneeling beside the cowboy. Blood had spread in a large circle over Hill's shirt from the wound in his chest. The sheriff had seen many a bullet wound, and he knew the reason that the doctor was not probing for it. It was clearly evident that Hill had only moments to live.

"What did you see, Jerry?" he asked softly.

Hill regarded the lawman with languid eyes. Running his tongue over his dry lips, he said in a faltering voice, "When I was hit, your . . . dad knelt down beside me. Vic Devlin was stompin' back and forth, shoutin' orders. Your dad . . . your dad picked up . . . my gun to use on Devlin, but . . . he was too slow. Devlin shot him, Tug."

"You recognized Vic Devlin, Jerry?" Farrell asked, surprised.

Hill nodded slowly. "Saw . . . a wanted poster on him."

Feeling a cold fury course through his body, Tug Farrell dashed out of the bank and ran up the street to his horse. Just as he vaulted into the saddle, he saw his deputy riding in from a side street. The sheriff filled him in on what had happened, and Harlon Stang was shocked.

"Maybe if I'd been here, I could have done something," he said. "I was out at the Anderson place, talking to Jimmy Anderson about some rustled cattle."

Shaking his head, Farrell told him, "It's not your fault. But I want you to take over here, 'cause I'm going after Vic Devlin." He was about to spur his horse, when he added, "Do me a favor, Harlon. See to it that my pop's body is taken care of."

"You can count on me, Tug."

Vengeance burned in Sheriff Tug Farrell as he followed Vic Devlin's trail, but although he was determined to catch up with the murderous outlaw, realistically he knew that Devlin and his men had a considerable lead. He had gone some ten miles north of Denver when he saw up ahead a horse grazing alongside the road. As he drew closer, he could make out the form of a man lying in the dust. Reaching the spot, the lawman slid from the saddle and looked down at the dead outlaw lying beside a money bag from the Denver Community Bank.

Rifling through the dead man's pockets, Farrell found papers that showed him to be Ernest Osgood from Hannibal, Missouri. He then stood and gazed at the northern horizon, saying aloud, "Well, Devlin, you must really be in a hurry to leave a sack full of money lying here with your dead partner. You're too far ahead of me for me to catch you, but I'm making you a promise. You killed my dad, and I'm going to kill you. You won't elude me for long. You can bet your last dollar on it."

Draping Ernie Osgood's body over the outlaw's horse, the sheriff headed back for Denver. He would deliver the money to the bank, take the body to the undertaker for burial, then ride to the Warren ranch. Maybe the gang member the Warrens were holding could tell him where Devlin was headed.

It was early afternoon when Sheriff Tug Farrell rode onto Paul Warren's ranch. As he drew near the house, he could see Warren and his son standing beside their hay wagon, and underneath the vehicle, still tied to the wheels, lay the outlaw. Warren and Danny waved at the lawman as he rode into their yard, and Opal and Darlene came out of the house to greet him as well.

Farrell dismounted and commented, "Looks like you've made sure he wouldn't get away."

"We were determined about that," Danny said proudly. "Did you catch the others, Sheriff?"

"Five of them are dead, son," Farrell replied slowly. "The leader, whose name is Vic Devlin, got away, and one of his cronies is with him."

"Vic Devlin!" exclaimed Warren. "So you were right, this really was the Vic Devlin gang."

"Yep. Apparently your friend under the wagon kept his mouth shut. Has he given you his name?"

"No," answered Warren. "He doesn't have much to say"—he smiled wryly—"although he seems to have a mighty big headache."

"His boss is going to have more than a headache when I catch up to him," Farrell growled, punching his fist into his palm. Noting the bewildered expressions on the Warrens' faces, he explained, "They robbed both banks at the same time, and there was a lot of shooting.

Several townspeople have been killed . . . including my father. Devlin himself shot Pop through the head."

The Warrens were stunned and quickly offered their sympathy.

Farrell stepped beside the wagon and knelt so he could face the trussed-up outlaw. "Did you hear what I just said, mister?"

Herb Frederick twisted his head slowly and looked the sheriff in the eye. "Yeah, I heard," he retorted.

His voice icy, Farrell declared, "Now, I know all about this so-called code of honor between you scummy outlaws, but you're going to break that code as of this minute, pal. First I want to know your name, and then I want to know where Devlin is headed. Time is of the essence, so I don't have much patience. And I'm warning you: If you don't tell me what I want to know easily, you're gonna regret it. 'Cause one way or another you *are* gonna tell me!"

Herb Frederick glared insolently at the lawman. "I ain't tellin' you nothin'," he rasped.

Farrell assessed the way the outlaw was tied to the wheels, realizing it would wrench his body severely if the wagon were to be moved. His temper short, he sighed and said, "Okay, pal. Have it your way."

The muscular sheriff stood and stepped to the back of the vehicle, then pushed it forward about three feet. Frederick's body twisted grotesquely and lifted off the ground at the same time. He howled in pain. Farrell pushed the wagon some more.

Frederick screamed loudly, begging Farrell to ease off. Holding one wheel so the vehicle could not roll back and drop the outlaw to the ground, the lawman leaned down and snapped, "I told you time is of the essence, mister. I want some answers, and I want them now. You either spit them out, or I'll push this wagon all over the ranch."

"No! Please!" gasped Frederick, suspended two feet off the ground. "My arms and legs are about to twist clear off my body!"

"I would say that's close to being true," Farrell threatened. "You want it to happen?"

"No!" cried the outlaw, gritting his teeth.

"Okay, then, what's your name?"

Frederick still did not answer. The ropes holding the outlaw were wrapped around both wheels and spokes, and with each further movement of the wheels, the pressure became more severe on the man's wrists and ankles. To show he meant business, Farrell pushed the buckboard ahead a few more inches.

The outlaw clenched his teeth in agony, sucking in air.

"I said, what's your name?" growled the sheriff.

"Herb Frederick!" bawled the outlaw.

"Good! Now we're getting somewhere. Tell me quick, where's Devlin headed?"

"Cheyenne," came the answer. "Please! Let me down and I'll tell you anything you want to know!"

The sheriff immediately complied. When Frederick's back was once again resting on the ground, Farrell snarled, "Okay, I'm listening."

Breathing hard, Frederick asked, "Do you know which of Devlin's men is with him?"

"No. I can only tell you that it's not Ernest Osgood. I found Osgood dead on the road about ten miles north of town. He'd been shot while they were making their getaway. Oh, yeah, you might want to know that four of your other pals are dead, the ones who tried robbing the Community Bank. But go ahead, I'm still listening."

"Okay, okay. Vic's headed for San Francisco. He's gonna catch the next train headed that way after he gets to Cheyenne."

"San Francisco? What's he going to do in San Francisco?"

"He's got plenty of money stashed in a bank there, and he plans to give up bank robbin' and open a saloon and casino."

Farrell became pensive, thinking about this information. He suddenly realized that Vic Devlin and his cohort would no doubt board the same train that he himself had been planning to take for Sacramento: The outlaws had ample time to reach Cheyenne by Friday, and the train went on to San Francisco after it left Sacramento. He gazed toward town. *Well, Devlin,* he thought to himself, *I'm going to have a little surprise waiting for you.*

The sun was casting long shadows when Farrell arrived back in Denver with his handcuffed prisoner. As he sat filling his deputy in on everything that had happened, the door opened and Clyde Towner entered the office. Closing the door behind him, the federal man approached the desk where Farrell sat, and said solemnly, "Tug, I'm so sorry about your dad. Please accept my deepest sympathy."

"Thank you, Clyde," the sheriff responded, his heart heavy.

"May I talk to you for a few minutes?" asked Towner.

"Certainly. Have a seat." When the chief U.S. marshal had done so, Farrell looked at him and queried, "What can I do for you, Clyde?"

"I understand you brought in one of the Devlin gang."

"Yep. Says his name's Herb Frederick."

"I need to talk to him."

"Sure. What about?"

"I've got to find out if he knows where Devlin might be headed. As soon as I can free up a federal marshal, I want to put him on Devlin's trail."

"I already squeezed that information out of him," said Farrell. "Devlin and his last gang member are on their way to Cheyenne."

"Cheyenne?"

"Yep. They're planning to catch the same train I'm taking day after tomorrow to California. They're headed for San Francisco. I'm going to Sacramento." Farrell smiled grimly. "But I'm going to foil their plans and nab them either at the Cheyenne depot or after they're on the train." He paused, then asked, "Did you hear that it was Devlin himself who shot my father?"

"No, I didn't," replied Towner.

"Well, I want him, Clyde. I want him real bad. And you can rest assured, I'll get him."

Clyde Towner leaned forward in his chair and said, "Tug, I can't blame you for wanting to get your hands on the man who killed your dad, but Vic Devlin is wanted by federal authorities. You'll have to leave the pursuit and capture of Devlin to my office. I'll have a man on his trail as soon as I can get one."

Farrell bristled, and a sudden flush of blood brightened his cheeks. "Clyde, that skunk killed my father. Put a bullet between his eyes. Don't tell me I can't go after him."

"Federal law is bigger than county law!" Towner forcefully reminded the lawman. "You'll have to stay out of the way, Tug. This was a federal case before Devlin rode into Denver today."

Farrell's big fist came down hard on the desktop. "Clyde," he said heatedly, "you're not making sense! While you're still looking for a federal marshal to go after him, Devlin will get away!"

Clyde Towner rose halfway out of his chair and planted his elbows on the desk, putting his face close to Farrell's. With flashing eyes he countered, "Well, Tug, my friend, I offered you a U.S. marshal's badge, but you turned it down!" Holding the big man's gaze, Towner eased back in the chair.

Tug Farrell desperately wanted to be the man to bring Vic Devlin to justice, and he began weighing his options. He concluded quickly that with his father dead, there was nothing holding him in Denver. He was now free to travel. He toyed with the ends of his mustache for a moment, then responded, "All right. I'll take the commission."

Towner was a bit taken aback by such a quick answer. His mouth fell open. "Just like that?"

"Just like that."

"Without even thinking it over?"

"I did think it over."

"Well, it seems a bit rash—and to be honest, I think I'd better rescind that offer. I mean, a couple of days ago when I sat in this same chair and offered you the commission, you said no. What worries me now is that you only want it so you can be the one to go after Devlin. We can't have a man wearing a U.S. marshal's badge just so he can carry out personal vendettas. Frankly, Tug, I'm afraid with revenge burning in your blood like it is, you'll kill Devlin on sight. No, I think I'd better withdraw my offer."

"Now, wait a minute!" blared Farrell. "What reason did I give you for turning down the offer? Was it not that I couldn't leave Pop here alone?"

"Well, yes . . . that's what you said."

"Okay, Clyde, Pop's dead."

Towner slowly shook his head. "I don't know, Tug. If it was *my* father Devlin had shot between the eyes, I'm not sure that I wouldn't want to go after him for personal reasons." He paused and rubbed his neck. "Tell you what. Why don't you let me get you the commission, then put you on a case that's already being worked by another federal marshal. That'll free him to go after Devlin."

Farrell frowned. Regarding the chief U.S. marshal coolly, he demanded, "Have you ever known me to disgrace this badge on my chest, Clyde?"

"Of course not."

"Then don't you think I deserve a little consideration here? I give you my word: I will not go after Devlin for personal retaliation. If I'm wearing a United States marshal's badge, I'll conduct myself accordingly —but I want to be the man to bring Devlin in for trial."

Towner started to say something, then cocked his head and appraised Farrell. "Tell me, Tug, why are you making a trip to Sacramento in the first place?"

Farrell grinned slyly and picked up the September 30 issue of the *Rocky Mountain Sentinel*. Before handing it to Towner, he asked, "Do you remember the discussion we had the other day when you were in here with Richards and Ingram?"

"Yes. The Raven Morrow-Clete Hobbs story. Why?"

Placing the newspaper in Towner's hand with it folded to the article about the pair arrested near Sacramento for running a slave operation in a gold mine, Farrell suggested, "Here. Read this."

When Clyde Towner had finished reading the article, Farrell told him of going to the mine and finding that Raven Morrow and Clete Hobbs had escaped. He concluded, "If I'm right, and those two out there in the Sacramento jail prove to be Raven and Hobbs, I'll see the governor about extradition papers. If you get me the commission as a U.S. marshal, I'll have the authority to bring them back for trial myself."

Excitement showed in Clyde Towner's eyes. Smiling broadly, he said, "Tug, nothing would make me happier than to see those two cold-blooded killers hang on a Colorado gallows for the crimes they committed here!"

"You willing to trust me? I mean, that I'll keep my word and go after Vic Devlin as a U.S. marshal, and not as Maynard Farrell's son?"

Standing up, Towner grinned and replied, "I'll trust you, all right. First thing in the morning, I'll wire Washington. With my recommendation and your record as a tough and resourceful lawman, there's no question you'll get the commission. We should have the answer within a few hours after I send the wire. I'll see you in the morning."

The sheriff turned to his deputy, who had sat quietly listening during the entire exchange. "Well, Harlon, what about you? Do you think you can handle the job of interim sheriff of Denver County until a new man is elected?"

Stang grinned. "I think so. After all, I've had the best teacher in the world."

"Good. I'll call the council members together for an

emergency session tonight. Hopefully they'll agree with us."

At midmorning the next day, Maynard Farrell and the other townsmen who had been killed in the bank robberies were buried. Standing in the cemetery beside the newly turned mound of earth, Tug Farrell keenly felt the loss of his father. But at the same time there was eager anticipation within him at the prospect of going after his father's killer—not to mention Raven Morrow and Clete Hobbs.

Late in the afternoon, a wire arrived from Washington, confirming the approval of Tug Farrell's appointment as United States marshal. Another meeting of the county officials was held, and Farrell officially resigned as sheriff of Denver County, while Harlon Stang was appointed interim sheriff. Before the same group, Chief United States Marshal Clyde Towner administered the oath to Tug Farrell and proudly pinned the new badge on his chest.

Clapping his new superior on the shoulder, Tug Farrell told Towner, "I promise you that this new badge doesn't change the man wearing it; it just changes my jurisdiction."

# Chapter Six

At the county jail in Sacramento, California, Sheriff Bob Sovern sat behind his desk talking with his two deputies. In his early forties—nearly twice the age of the deputies, both in their mid-twenties—the sheriff pushed back the hat he wore nearly all the time in order to cover his bald pate, then reached for a cigar from the humidor on his desk. He shoved the stogie into his mouth, which was completely obscured by his thick, bushy mustache, and bit off the end, then spit it into his wastebasket.

"What do you boys think about this news from this Sheriff Farrell?" the thick-bodied lawman asked.

Deputy Ed Willis settled his likewise chunky frame into his chair across from the sheriff and declared, "Sure seems like the two we're holding are the same ones Farrell's described."

"I agree," the other deputy, John Way, put in from where he stood with his back to the window. The slender, curly-haired Way kept his eyes fixed on Sovern, and the backlighting made his cheeks appear even more hollow than usual.

Sheriff Sovern flared a match and lit his cigar. He puffed hard to get the cigar going, then said, "Bring in those two prisoners—but one at a time. I'm not going to tell them about Farrell coming. I want to see if I can make them admit their true identities before he arrives."

Ed Willis's face flushed, turning as red as his hair

67

and masking his hundreds of freckles. "Oh-oh," he said weakly.

"What's the matter?" queried the sheriff.

Clearing his throat, Willis replied, "I wasn't aware you wanted to keep Farrell's coming a secret. I told Hoffman—or should I say Hobbs?—about it when I took the male prisoners their breakfast a little while ago."

Sovern chewed on the cigar, blinking against the smoke that was drifting into his eyes. Shaking his head, he breathed, "Not your fault, Ed. You didn't know." Turning to Way, he asked, "Did you say anything about it to the woman when you fed the females?"

"Nope."

"Good. Okay, here's what we'll do. We'll bring her in first, and I'll apply a little pressure. If she breaks down and admits who she is, it'll be a feather in my cap, and I can use her confession as leverage on her pal afterward." He leaned back in his chair and hooked his thumbs into his suspenders. "If I can get them both to come clean, we'll get a reporter in here and tell him the whole story. Come next election, my having squeezed the truth out of those two will help swing a big hammer toward me retaining my job."

John Way chuckled, "That's good thinking. The people like to feel confident that they have a man in office who knows how to deal with criminals."

"John told me you got a second telegram, saying Farrell is now a U.S. marshal," spoke up Ed Willis.

"Mm-hmm. Came late yesterday afternoon after you'd gone home."

"You don't suppose he became a federal man just so he could be the one to take that pair back to Denver, do you?" asked Way.

"I don't know," replied Sovern. "The telegram was quite brief. He just wanted me to know that he'd be taking them back himself."

"Well," John Way said as he walked toward the door leading to the cells, "since I'm in charge of the women's side of the jail, I'll go bring that beautiful creature in here." He sighed. "Sure is hard to believe she's a criminal—especially a murderer."

As Way disappeared through the door Sovern puffed on his cigar and commented, "She sure is some looker, that female."

"Yeah," agreed Willis, "the kind men will kill for."

Sovern and Willis were still discussing Rita Marston's captivating beauty when the door opened and the subject of their conversation entered the office with Deputy John Way behind her. Though she was clad in a dismal gray dress provided by the Sacramento County jail, she looked so radiant that she might well have been garbed in the most exquisite of evening gowns.

Her long black hair swirled down both sides of her face, tumbling over her shoulders, and while there was a certain hardness in her dark, mysterious eyes, there was also something magnetic about them. They could cast a spell on a man in quick order.

The enchanting brunette stood for a moment in the doorway, assessing the situation—and obviously letting the men assess her in turn. Then, with her wrists handcuffed in front of her, she slowly sashayed toward the sheriff's desk, her full lips curving into a come-hither smile. "Good morning, gentlemen."

Both Sovern and Willis stood up and, gesturing toward his deputy's chair, the sheriff offered, "Please sit down."

Glancing at the lawman provocatively, the woman calling herself Rita Marston sat as requested, then gazed at the three men ringed around her.

The sheriff eased onto his chair and stared at her with the cigar clamped between his teeth. He shoved it to one side, about to speak, but before he uttered a word, the brunette glanced up at Way, then remarked, "This handsome deputy said you wanted to have a chat with me, Sheriff. Are you by any chance going to tell me why our trial has suddenly been postponed? You've been awfully secretive about it, don't you think?"

Ignoring her remarks, Sovern looked her in the eye

and asked without prelude, "What's your real name, ma'am?"

"Why, Sheriff," she cooed, leaning closer to the desk, "I've already told you. My name is Rita Marston."

Feeling uncomfortable under her gaze, as if she had bewitched him, Sheriff Bob Sovern shook his head fervently. "You're not being honest with me, ma'am," he retorted. "Now, let's have the truth. What is your real name?"

"Rita Marston *is* my real name," she insisted. "Would you feel better if I lied and told you it was Florence Nightingale?"

Enthralled as he was by her beauty, Sovern was irritated by her insolence. "I have it on good authority that you are really Raven Morrow!" he snapped.

The woman tried to disguise her surprise, but a tiny muscle twitched in her left cheek. Obviously trying hard to maintain her demeanor, she said in a monotone, "I don't know about any Raven Morrow."

"I think you do, ma'am. What's more, your boyfriend is really Clete Hobbs—and the two of you are wanted for murder in Colorado. Seems you ran the same kind of operation there that I arrested you for a few weeks ago. Only in Colorado, you murdered several men in cold blood."

The color on the woman's cheeks paled, and her face looked as though it were carved from ivory. Then, regaining both her composure and her color, she batted her long eyelashes, rose from the chair, and sat on the edge of the desk. She leaned close to Sovern, and he found her closeness unsettling.

"Now, Sheriff," Raven Morrow breathed, reaching toward him with her shackled hands, "do I look like a cold-blooded killer to you?" She removed the cigar from his mouth and placed it in her own. Blowing a cloud of smoke at him, she then asked in a throaty voice, "Do I look like a cold-blooded *anything* to you?"

Sovern's bald scalp prickled underneath his hat, and his heart quickened pace. "Well, I . . . I did comment to my deputy a little while ago that it was hard to believe a woman as beautiful as you are could be so—"

"Could be so what? So interested in such a handsome sheriff?"

While Bob Sovern was swallowing hard, thinking that her laughter was as charming as everything else about her, Raven asked, "Now, where does this so-called proof come from that I'm this Raven Morrow?"

"From somebody who knows you personally," came Sovern's immediate response.

"Who?" Raven asked, blowing smoke in his face gently and letting him feel the warmth of her breath.

It came out before the sheriff was aware the name was on the tip of his tongue. "Tug Farrell."

"Tug Farrell?" she repeated. "I don't know any Tug Farrell. Who is he?"

"Sheriff of Denver, Colorado," breathed Sovern. "Uh, that is, he used to be. He's a U.S. marshal now, and he's on his way here to identify you."

Suddenly the lawman's mouth clamped shut. He was taken aback when he realized that he had been manipulated by his beautiful prisoner into revealing more than he had ever intended. Now the newspapers would never carry the story of how Sacramento County's Sheriff Bob Sovern had made his prisoner admit her true identity. His only hope at this point was to get the truth out of "Clarence Hoffman."

Glancing at his prisoner, he saw the fear in her eyes, although she covered it well with her forced bravado. He knew she was thinking that if she and her partner were extradited to Colorado, they would hang for their crimes. "Sit back in the chair," Sovern snapped at the brunette. As she obeyed, he rasped, "You can deny your identity all you want, but it won't do you any good once Farrell gets here."

"I don't know what you're talking about," she insisted, her voice now hard.

"Oh, you don't, eh? Well, I think the fact that you and your hoodlums were running virtually the same operation in the Sierras as you did in the Rockies is ample proof, Miss Morrow."

She sneered contemptuously at the sheriff and hissed, "You'll never catch the rest of the gang. You only nabbed me and my partner because you caught us off guard. Jack Bullard and the boys will never let you catch them."

"We killed five of your gang the day we moved in on your operation," Sovern reminded her. "Too bad the others weren't there. How many did Bullard have with him?"

"That's for me to know and you to wonder about," she replied tartly.

Sovern regarded her for a long moment. "You know, things could be better for you if you're pleasant and cooperative. I'll ask you again: Are you Raven Morrow?"

The woman's whole countenance stiffened, and she sat motionless, saying nothing.

Sovern sighed, stood up, and ordered, "Deputy Way, take *Miss Morrow* back to her cell."

Way nodded and took hold of her arm. "All right, let's go."

With catlike quickness, the prisoner leapt to her feet and, getting behind Way, threw her cuffed hands over his head, locking the chain links against his Adam's apple. The deputy gagged and choked as she held him fast with her strong arms. When the other two lawmen rushed to Way's defense, her eyes blazed and she threatened, "Get back, or I'll kill him! I swear, I'll kill him!"

But Bob Sovern ignored Raven's threat and sent a stiff punch to the side of her head, temporarily stunning her. She sagged to her knees, and Willis and Sovern slipped Way out of Raven's arms. Coughing and gagging, Way put his hands to his sore throat, struggling to get air into his lungs.

Sovern advised the deputy, "Next time, you better cuff her hands behind her. Come on, sit down for a few minutes."

John Way nodded and stumbled into the sheriff's chair, still coughing.

Turning to his other deputy, the sheriff told him, "Ed, you take her back to her cell. You've got a few more pounds over her than John does."

Ed Willis pulled Raven to her feet and helped her toward the door. Before they reached it, however, her head cleared, and without warning she jumped the deputy, clawing his face with her long fingernails. She was like a wildcat, snarling and screaming.

The sheriff spat out a string of curses and bounded across the room, pouncing on his prisoner. Jerking her away from Willis, his meaty hand grabbed her shoulder and he spun her around. Before she could use her nails on him, he chopped her jaw with a powerful right cross, and this time she went down in a heap, unconscious.

Deputy Ed Willis staggered into the washroom and, pouring water from a pitcher into a basin, soaked a towel and then held it to his scratched face. Shaking his head, Sheriff Sovern told his deputy, "Hard to believe one dainty-looking female could have wreaked such havoc on the deputies of Sacramento." He sighed. "Well, I guess it's up to me to get her safely under lock and key."

Walking over to the limp form of Raven Morrow, the sheriff knelt and lifted her into his arms, then threw her over his shoulder like a sack of potatoes and carried her into the cell area. Since the Sacramento County jail presently had two female prisoners, the sheriff had placed them in cells that were in a different block from where the men were incarcerated.

As he passed the cell of the other woman prisoner and stepped into the adjacent one, the large and stout middle-aged woman stepped to the bars separating the two cells. Gripping the bars, Maude Esther Dodd commented, "I heard some ruckus goin' on out there, Sheriff. What happened?"

Raven was beginning to stir as he unceremoniously dumped her onto the cot. "She can tell you when she wakes up," Sovern replied while unlocking the handcuffs that circled her wrists. Raven rolled her head and moaned again as Sovern left the cell, slamming the door shut and locking it behind him.

Watching the lawman's retreating back as he returned to his office, Maude Esther Dodd silently mimicked his words, then sniffed derisively. She turned around and walked over to the bars and looked down at her beautiful neighbor, unconsciously running a hand through her straggly gray hair as she gazed at the woman's thick—albeit disheveled—black tresses.

The hard life Maude Esther had lived had taken its toll on her appearance, and her face had deep lines and wrinkles that made her look fifteen years older than the forty-five she really was. "Tough as boot leather and hard as marble," one judge had called her—a description she was proud of. She had been behind bars many times before, having a long criminal record of bank and stagecoach robberies, first with her late husband—who had been killed during a bank robbery—then with her two sons. The sons recently had been shot to death during a stagecoach holdup—the same one for which Maude Esther had been arrested for shooting and killing the driver. She now awaited trial in the Sacramento jail, and she knew she was going to hang for the crime. With her record, no jury would acquit her, and no judge would even consider passing a mere life sentence.

While Raven continued to stir on her bunk, the big woman crossed her cell to the small table beside her bunk and picked up the cigarette that she had rolled previously and stuck it between her lips. Striking a match with her thumbnail, she lit the cigarette dangling from the corner of her mouth, blew out a long stream of smoke, then sat down on her bunk and watched the young woman in the adjoining cell.

Raven finally opened her eyes several minutes later. Although it was obviously painful for her to do so, she sat up, holding her hands to her face. There were purple bruises on her jaw, which was somewhat swollen, and her long black hair hung over her eyes.

Maude Esther got off the cot and carried a small

stool close to the bars and sat on it. The battered brunette rubbed her jaw and shoved her hair back off her face, giving the big woman a quick glance.

"What happened, honey?" Maude Esther asked.

For response, Raven groaned, "I've got a headache. You got any powders?"

"Sure," her neighbor replied, rising from the stool. Rummaging through her reticule, which she had been allowed to keep in the cell, Maude Esther came up with the desired item and handed it through the bars. Raven thanked her, carried the small envelope to her washstand, and poured a portion of its contents into a tin cup that was already half-full of water. She drank it to the last drop, then plunked the cup on the table and staggered back to her bunk.

Looking at the portly woman through half-closed eyes, Raven muttered, "Maude Esther, I'm going to have to lie down for a little while. We'll talk later, okay?"

"Sure, honey. You just take it easy."

As Raven stretched out on her bunk, Maude Esther returned to her own and sat down. Puffing on the cigarette, she leaned back against the wall and stared vacantly into space.

Nearly an hour had passed when Raven Morrow sat up, lit a cigarillo, and looked through the bars toward her newfound friend. Returning to the stool by the bars, Maude Esther looked at her neighbor with concern and asked, "Feelin' any better?"

"Much."

"Now, tell me what happened, honey."

A slow tide of ruddy color crept over Raven Morrow's face and fire flashed in her eyes as she said, "That snake-bellied sheriff punched me a good one, that's what happened." Hanging the cigarillo in the corner of her mouth, she stood and adjusted the skirt of her dress, then sat down again.

"Well, that wasn't very gentlemanly of him," commented Maude Esther sarcastically. "What'd he do that for?"

"Oh," Raven said, grinning maliciously, "all I did was try to choke Deputy Way to death and claw Deputy Willis's eyes out."

The big woman snorted. "Why, I declare, dearie, that's sure nothin' for Sovern to get all upset about."

The two women howled with laughter. Then Raven's face sobered and she said softly, "Clete and I are in trouble, Maude Esther."

"How's that?"

"Remember that operation I told you I had going in Colorado about three years ago?"

"Yep."

"Well, we worked those kidnapped men plenty hard, and lots of them died. 'Course, we also had to flat out kill several of them who rebelled against the conditions and shoot down some for trying to escape." She laughed. "The law calls that kind of thing murder."

"Do tell," the buxom woman replied, chuckling.

"Anyway," proceeded Raven, "during the time we were getting rich from our operation, the sheriff in Denver began nosing around, concerned about all the men in the area who were disappearing. In order to divert his attention from our mine, I managed to wheedle myself into his life. The stupid chump fell in love with me—even asked me to marry him—having no idea that I was running the slave camp that he was trying so hard to find and close down. By leading him on, I was able to at least slow down his search."

"With your looks, sweetie, you could divert a train from its track and make it take a dirt road," remarked Maude Esther.

Raven laughed. "Why, thank you, Maude Esther." She paused, then continued, "At any rate, I knew I was really only buying time so we could get out of the mountain as much gold as possible. Finally we decided the sheriff was getting too close and had to die. I set up a trap for him, planning on blowing his brains out and dumping his body down a mine shaft, but it backfired.

To make a long story short, Farrell—that's his name, Tug Farrell—turned out to be a remarkably resourceful cuss, and before I knew it, my gang was wiped out and Clete and I had to escape in a hurry."

Maude Esther interrupted, "Something tells me you were just as resourceful as Farrell."

"To a degree—although Mother Nature came to our rescue. We had prepared a secret escape shaft in the mountain in case of emergency, but Farrell plugged up the trapdoor at the top of the shaft. Fortunately, an explosion that might have spelled our doom—'cause it caved in a good portion of the mountain—opened up a new way to escape. By a freak of nature, instead of Clete and me being trapped to die, we were able to get out and we made our way to California."

"And I know the rest of the story," Maude Esther remarked.

"All except for the part that has Clete and me in deep trouble. You see, Farrell's a U.S. marshal now, and he's apparently on his way here from Denver to identify Clete and me. Somehow he found out we didn't get killed in that mine explosion—and he also learned of our being in jail here. When he fingers us, we'll be taken back to Denver to face murder charges. They'll hang us for sure."

The portly woman shook her head, making her jowls flap. "Mercy me, little gal, you are indeed in a peck of trouble. The charges you're facin' here are practically nothin' compared to murder. Somehow you've got to get out of here before that Farrell guy shows up."

"You're telling me! But with every tick of the clock, that chance grows slimmer, Maude Esther," Raven pointed out. She looked around to make sure they were not being overheard, then confided, "I have no doubt that Jack Bullard is planning to break Clete and me out of here, but he's not going to try it until he can recruit some more men. Sovern and his posse really cut down our ranks. My fear is that Farrell will get here before Jack breaks us out."

"What are you gonna do if Jack *does* get you out?" asked Maude Esther.

"Head north to Canada. The boys and I were already making plans in that direction before Sovern moved in on us. The mine was about played out anyhow."

"Canada, eh?" Maude Esther breathed wistfully.

"Mm-hmm." Raven dropped her cigarillo on the floor and crushed it. "Several months ago I learned of a rich vein of gold that was discovered deep in the Selkirk Mountains in southern British Columbia. If Clete and I can just get out of here, that's where we're going."

Leaning closer to the bars, the big woman said, "Raven, honey, you know I'm in pretty bad trouble myself. Wouldn't surprise me if they're makin' a hangman's noose for me right now."

Raven nodded wordlessly.

"When you break out, will you take me with you?"

The beautiful woman's eyebrows rose in surprise. Then she smiled. "I hadn't thought of it before, but sure, Maude Esther. We'll be glad to take you with us. So you better start praying that Jack gets here before that stupid marshal does."

Clete Hobbs—calling himself Clarence Hoffman—was brought from his cell to Sheriff Bob Sovern's office with his hands carefully cuffed behind his back. Although the rawboned outlaw was still in his mid-thirties, he looked—and, he had to admit, sometimes felt—well into his forties. Deputy Ed Willis shoved the prisoner into the chair in front of the sheriff's desk, then flanked him on the other side from John Way.

The sheriff regarded Hobbs for a long moment, then said, "Deputy Willis has informed me that he told you about the expected arrival of U.S. Marshal Tug Farrell. Correct?"

"Yeah," the prisoner responded dully.

"Now, I'm not going to play games with you, mister. I know your real name is Clete Hobbs. If you'll own up to it, I'll see that things go a whole lot better for you."

Hobbs was shaken at the prospect of dying on a gallows in Colorado, and despite his best efforts, his craggy and worn face took on a haunted look. But he refused to give the lawmen the satisfaction of knowing how he felt, and he replied impassively, "You're barking up the wrong tree. I ain't Clete Hobbs. My name is Clarence Hoffman."

It pleased Hobbs that Sheriff Sovern was clearly frustrated in his attempt to gain the truth. Pulling his mouth into a thin line, the lawman growled, "Okay, Mr. Hobbs, have it your way. You can face Tug Farrell with no help from me." Lifting his eyes to Willis, he muttered, "Take him back to his cell."

When the cell door clanged shut behind Clete Hobbs, he sat down on his bunk and lit a cigarette with shaky hands. Blowing smoke toward the ceiling, Hobbs swore under his breath. He wished he could talk to Raven. She was the brains of the outfit, and he would feel better if he could discuss the situation with her. He was certain that Jack Bullard and the rest of the gang would break them out—although less certain than he had been when they were first arrested.

*You've got to spring us out of here soon, Jack,* he said to himself, *before Farrell arrives.*

At an old abandoned farmhouse a few miles south of Sacramento, two ragged-looking men in their thirties sat in the kitchen, passing a whiskey bottle back and forth between them. Mack Dugan scratched at his four-day growth of beard and mumbled, "I sure hope Jack'll come back with some good news. We gotta spring Raven and Clete outta that stinkin' jail before they go to trial, 'cause there ain't no way we could bust 'em outta some state penitentiary."

Earl Penrod took a swig of whiskey and drawled, "I wouldn't mind puttin' a bullet through that stinkin' sheriff's head myself. But just three of us movin' in to break Raven and Clete outta that jail is a little risky."

"I know, but if Jack don't come up with some other

fellas, we ain't gonna have no choice. We sure ain't
nothin' without Raven."

Penrod let out a long sigh and started to say something, when they heard hoofbeats outside. Penrod's
hand went to his holster as he hurried to the window
and peered out. "It's Jack," he told his cohort, relaxing.
"But he's alone."

Jack Bullard dismounted by the back porch. A
mountain of a man, he stood six-feet-six and weighed
almost three hundred pounds. He had huge shoulders
and arms like tree trunks, and his thick beard and his
salt-and-pepper hair covered his neck both back and
front.

"So how'd it go?" asked Penrod as Bullard bowled
through the door.

"Pretty good, I think," came the answer in a deep,
rumbly voice. "My little jaunt to Placerville may just
have been worth it. Got six or seven men showin' real
interest in joinin' the gang. They're gonna let me know
within a few days."

"I sure hope it's *very* few, Jack," spoke up Mack
Dugan. "The paper said the trial was postponed, but it
didn't say for how long." He scratched his beard again.
"Funny. It also didn't say why."

Bullard grunted, and the other men exchanged
glances. It was always hard to tell if the sound was the
huge man's laugh or whether he was angry. "It don't
matter why; it just gives us more time to get 'em out.
And you can count on it that one way or the other, we'll
get 'em out, 'cause I ain't lettin' Raven go to prison."

Penrod and Dugan glanced at each other again.
They knew that although Jack Bullard had never voiced
it to any of the gang—and he had never worked up the
courage to tell her—he was head over heels in love with
Raven Morrow.

# Chapter Seven

Carrying a small suitcase, U.S. Marshal Tug Farrell arrived at Denver's Union Station for the three-hour ride to Cheyenne, Wyoming. Chief United States Marshal Clyde Towner, at the station to see Farrell off, was standing beside the train, waiting for his new marshal. As Farrell approached, Towner asked, "Did you learn who the guy with Devlin is?"

"Yeah. Mel Stuart," responded Farrell. "Herb Frederick looked at all his dead cronies awaiting burial, and by process of elimination he fingered Stuart. Unfortunately, his description of him was pretty general—medium height, medium build, and medium-brown hair—but I doubt I'll have any trouble identifying him. He'll be the dude who sticks close to Devlin." The lawman patted his pocket. "And fortunately I have this wanted poster with Devlin's picture on it. I'm sure glad you had it in your files." Grinning, he added, "And since Devlin doesn't know what I look like, it'll give me a distinct advantage."

"You're sure you can handle this without letting your personal feelings get in the way, Tug?" Towner asked.

"Yes, sir. I won't say that I haven't had thoughts of how pleasurable it would be to kill Devlin a half-inch at a time, but I'll honor this badge you pinned on me. If I come back with Devlin dead, it'll be only because he wouldn't let me take him alive."

The train whistle sounded, and the new marshal smiled. "Well, Clyde, that's my cue."

The two federal men shook hands, and Tug Farrell boarded the train. Finding a seat, he made himself comfortable, then removed the folded poster from his shirt pocket and opened it up. As he studied the photograph of outlaw Victor Devlin, wanted dead or alive for bank robbery and murder, Farrell mumbled under his breath, "I'm going to get you, Devlin. That's a solemn vow. And I'm more than half-hoping you resist arrest, 'cause I'll be more than happy to bring you back in a coffin." Folding the poster and putting it into his pocket, the U.S. marshal leaned back in the seat and tipped his hat over his eyes.

As the train rolled northward, Tug Farrell's thoughts went from Vic Devlin to the couple waiting behind bars at the Sacramento County jail. Visualizing the moment he would look upon their faces, he decided it would be a little like seeing a couple of ghosts—after all, he had lived the past three years thinking they were dead. But soon all the thoughts swirling around in the lawman's mind vanished as the steady click of the wheels and the rhythmic sway of the coach lulled him to sleep.

Opening his eyes with a start, Farrell was pulled from his deep sleep by the call of the conductor, who was moving through the car, making an announcement. When he focused on what the trainman was saying, the lawman was surprised to discover that he had slept virtually the entire ride, for they would be arriving in Cheyenne in twenty minutes.

When the train finally pulled into the windswept Wyoming town, Farrell peered through the window. Cheyenne was a wild town, its dusty streets lined with tents serving as saloons and dance halls, interspersed with several clapboard buildings. The new marshal had once read that there were seven shootings a week, on the average—one for every day of the week.

The big engine chugged to a halt, its bell clanging and steam billowing. Suitcase in hand, Farrell stepped

off the train onto the platform and looked around. On
the other side of the platform, beyond the depot building, stood another train—which he was sure was the one
that would take him to California. Walking over to a
conductor standing alongside the train, the lawman had
his assumption confirmed.

He stared at the train, wondering if perhaps Devlin
and Stuart were already on board. Aside from the locomotive and coal car, it consisted of five passenger cars
and a caboose. Pulling out his pocket watch, he saw that
there was almost an hour left before departure. He
decided that it was unlikely the outlaws would just wait
on the train like sitting ducks until it left, preferring to
board at the last minute.

Tug Farrell walked through the milling crowd, his
eyes darting back and forth as he searched the faces of
the men. As he reached the front of the depot without
spotting his quarry, it crossed Farrell's mind that it
would be best not to advertise that he was a lawman. He
removed the badge from his chest and slipped it into a
vest pocket, deciding to just leave it there until Devlin
and Stuart were in his custody.

Heading back toward his train, the big, tall federal
man walked at an easy pace and kept up a constant vigil
for Devlin and Stuart. Periodically he pulled out his
pocket watch, and soon it was less than a half hour
before departure time.

Farrell paced the platform alongside the waiting
train, keeping a sharp eye for the two outlaws. When it
was down to ten minutes before the train would pull
out, Farrell's nerves began to tighten. He dared not
leave Cheyenne without capturing Devlin and Stuart
or at least knowing that they were on the train.

Soon the conductor appeared on the platform of
the first car, chatting with a man whom Farrell guessed
was a railroad official. The conductor would shortly be
calling for the last stragglers to board. The U.S. marshal
checked his watch. Six minutes to go.

Farrell suddenly leapt onto the platform and
pushed past the two railroad men into the first of the

five passenger cars. Time was short. Perhaps the two outlaws had boarded the train early after all—or had managed to slip on without his seeing them. He had to know. Scanning faces, he walked through the first car but saw neither man. He passed into the second, then the third, and finally the fourth. By the time he emerged through the front door of the fifth car, panic was rising within him. Devlin and Stuart were not on the train, and it was going to leave in another four minutes. He jumped down onto the platform and resumed pacing back and forth alongside the train. Then he realized that it was entirely possible that while he had been going through the cars, the outlaws had gotten on behind him without his knowledge. He started rushing toward the front of the train, peering up at the windows as he ran.

On the street in front of the depot, Vic Devlin and Mel Stuart alighted from a carriage carrying new suitcases. Well-groomed, they were both dressed sharply in three-piece suits and with derby hats perched jauntily on their heads.

The muscular Devlin said to his cohort, "You go ahead and board the train and grab a couple of seats. And don't let 'em leave without me. I'm goin' across the street to that tobacco shop and get me some cigarillos."

Stuart nodded and headed toward the train. The big engine was puffing steam, and the bell started to clang. The third car being the most convenient, Stuart made a beeline for it, elbowing his way through the crowded platform.

In his rush to the train, he collided with Tug Farrell. Being the lighter man, Stuart was knocked off balance, but he was saved from falling when the lawman reached out and grasped his arm. The outlaw's derby was jarred loose and sailed to the ground.

"Excuse me, sir," Farrell said as he steadied Stuart, then bent down and picked up the hat. "I'm afraid I wasn't looking."

"No, it was *my* fault," Stuart declared expansively,

taking the proffered hat from Farrell's hand and dropping it back on his head. "I was in a hurry to get on the train, and wasn't payin' attention. No harm done."

The whistle suddenly blew, and the conductor, who stood on the lowest step of the front passenger car, shouted, "All aboard! All aboard!"

Mel Stuart dashed into the third car.

Tug Farrell stood there, at his wits' end. He needed to be on the train headed for Sacramento, but he also had to find and arrest Vic Devlin and his cohort—and there was no guarantee that they had in fact boarded. The whistle blew again. A shot of steam blasted from the locomotive, and the giant wheels began to roll. The U.S. marshal was forced to make a decision.

Then suddenly it was made for him. A stocky man in a gray pin-striped suit and derby hat was running toward the train, and then he hopped on the first car. Though Vic Devlin had improved his appearance considerably, Farrell had no doubt it was he. Heaving a sigh of relief, he ran alongside the rolling train and jumped onto the steps of the fifth and last car.

As Farrell entered the car he noted that it was almost full. He took a seat on the aisle next to an elderly woman who turned and gave him a friendly smile before turning back to the window. The marshal decided to wait until the train was out of Cheyenne and up to full speed before moving up to the first car, where he had seen Vic Devlin board. Since full speed was about forty-five miles an hour, it was unlikely that the outlaw would try jumping from the train to escape.

Rubbing his chin, Farrell wondered why Devlin was traveling alone. Where was Mel Stuart? Relaxing somewhat, he told himself it was all right. The man he really wanted was Devlin. He could trail Stuart later.

He pictured Devlin in his mind as he had just seen him—well-dressed and well-fed. Farrell wondered if the money the killer had used to buy his new suit was Maynard Farrell's. Rage seared through the lawman. It would be a pleasure to tear off both Devlin's arms and beat him to death with them.

Tug Farrell forced himself to view his assignment with professional detachment, figuring out how to capture Devlin aboard the train without getting any of the passengers hurt. It would take some careful planning. First the marshal would have to see just where the outlaw was sitting in the coach. Once that fact was known, he would have to improvise and make the best move at the right time.

Vic Devlin decided that boarding the first passenger car had made things easier for him: He would have to move in only one direction through the train to locate his partner. Leaving his seat in the first car, he passed to the second, noting that it—like the first—was completely full and his partner was not there. When he stepped into the third car, he spotted Stuart immediately. He was seated about halfway back by a window, on Devlin's right, but the aisle seat was occupied by a rather large middle-aged woman. Stuart had apparently been unable to find them seats together, and the only vacant seat was on the aisle four rows in front of where Stuart was seated.

Devlin walked down the aisle, swaying in rhythm with the car's motion. Stopping beside the woman who sat next to his partner, Devlin looked past her and growled at Stuart, "I thought you were gonna make 'em hold the train till I got on."

"I tried arguin' with the conductor," Stuart said defensively, "but he was a huffy so-and-so and told me they couldn't hold up the train for nobody. Then I saw you dartin' toward us, so I let it go."

"Okay," Devlin conceded.

Devlin then bent down to look the heavyset woman in the eye. "Excuse me, ma'am," he said, his voice wheedling. "I wonder if you'd do me and my friend a favor?"

Scowling at him, the woman retorted, "If you're going to ask me to find another seat so you can sit next to him, save your breath."

Devlin wanted to shake her, but maintaining his

slightly obsequious manner, he told her, "It seems that you are travelin' alone, ma'am, so what difference should it make to you if you sit in another seat? My pal and I need to talk business." Gesturing over his shoulder, he added, "There's a seat on the aisle just four rows away."

"Take it yourself," the woman snapped.

Vic Devlin had to force himself not to slug her, but he knew that an outlaw on the dodge did not need to draw attention to himself. He glared at her for a few seconds, then said to Stuart, "We'll get together later." With that, he pivoted and walked back to the coach's only vacant seat.

The Union Pacific train had been out of Cheyenne for about an hour when U.S. Marshal Tug Farrell decided it was time to walk to the first passenger car and capture Vic Devlin. As he made his way forward, he realized he would have to go to the very front of that car, then head back in the opposite direction so he could see the faces of the travelers. Picking Devlin out from behind would be quite difficult, if not impossible.

People were moving about in the aisle as Farrell strolled to the front of car number one, then slowly turned around and gazed indifferently at the faces of the occupants. His pulse quickened. Devlin was not here! Worry scratched at his mind, and he wondered if somehow the outlaw had gotten off the train before it was out of Cheyenne. He told himself this could not be, that for some reason Devlin had changed coaches. Maybe the car had been full. With people up and moving about, it was hard to tell if all the seats were taken.

Keeping a casual air about him, the federal man moved to the second car and paused to scan the faces of its occupants. Again no Vic Devlin. As he stood on the platform between the second and third cars he remembered that he had seen a gray pin-striped suit in number three. He had not expected Devlin to be in that car, so the suit had not really attracted his attention. The wind plucked at his hat while he took a quick look through the window in the door. Instantly he picked out Devlin seated on the aisle a few rows from the front. His heart pounded as he pulled open the door and stepped into the car.

With a nonchalance that he did not feel, Farrell leaned against the wall at the front of the car, hoping he appeared to be just breaking the monotony of sitting. Vic Devlin looked up, his gaze settling on Farrell, and the marshal's scalp tightened. As far as he knew, Devlin had never seen his face and did not know who he was. If he had, and he was recognizing him now, Farrell would have to act fast. His muscles tensed, then eased when the outlaw looked away without showing any glimmer of recognition.

Tug Farrell stood motionless, staring at the man who had killed his father. A vivid picture of Maynard Farrell's dead face, the bullet hole between his eyes, flashed into the lawman's mind. He figuratively shook his head to clear the horrific image, fingering the badge in his vest pocket to jolt him back to reality and restrain him from leaping onto the outlaw and tearing him limb from limb. The law that backed his badge stated that the criminal was to be punished by the people . . . not by their appointed representative, the man who wore the badge.

Quickly Farrell hatched a plan to apprehend his man without endangering any of the passengers in the car. Directly behind Devlin sat a young man in his early twenties. Farrell needed his seat.

The big lawman sauntered down the aisle to the young passenger. Taking the badge from his vest pocket, he flashed it at the young man, placing a finger over his mouth to signal him to keep quiet. From the corner of his eye, Farrell noticed that several other passengers saw what was going on and watched intently to see what was happening.

The young man behind Devlin got the message. He stood up without a word and hurried to the rear of the car, then out the doorway, giving Farrell his seat. The lawman felt lucky that the elderly woman in the window seat next to him was fast asleep—otherwise he might have had to calm her, giving himself away.

After pulling a pair of handcuffs from a coat pocket, Farrell then drew his Colt .45 and cocked it. He pressed the muzzle against the back of Vic Devlin's seat and, leaning forward, told the unsuspecting outlaw in a steely voice, "I'm U.S. Marshal Tug Farrell, Devlin, and this is a cocked Colt .45 in your back."

The outlaw's body went rigid.

"You are under arrest for bank robbery and murder. I want you to slowly stand up and put your hands behind your back." His voice even colder, Farrell breathed into the outlaw's ear, "Incidentally, the old man you shot between the eyes in the Denver bank was my father, so I'd really appreciate it if you'd resist arrest so I can blow you into eternity."

Sweat beaded Vic Devlin's brow as he obeyed Farrell's command and stood in the aisle with his hands behind him. Farrell clamped a cuff on Devlin's right wrist, the ratchet clicking loudly as he cinched it down tight, and then he leaned over and relieved the outlaw of his revolver, jamming it under his own belt. Farrell was about to snap the other cuff on his own wrist when a man across the aisle shouted, "Look out, lawman!"

Farrell's head whipped around. A well-dressed passenger a few seats back had just climbed over the large-bodied woman sleeping in the aisle seat and was drawing his gun, coming toward him. Suddenly a booted foot shot out, tripping the man and sending him sprawling while his revolver slipped from his fingers and disappeared under one of the seats.

Vic Devlin took advantage of the distraction and swung at Farrell, but the lawman ducked the punch and slammed a rock-hard fist into the outlaw's jaw. Devlin staggered backward, bounced off the shoulder of a passenger, then hit the floor.

Swearing profusely, Mel Stuart righted himself and charged, fists swinging. When Stuart first tried to attack, the marshal did not realize that the man was Devlin's cohort, thinking that perhaps some misguided passen-

ger—not realizing the situation—had deemed himself
Devlin's rescuer. But that was obviously not the case,
and Farrell did not hesitate putting all his weight behind the punch he shot into Stuart's chin, staggering
him. He was about to give the man a second one when
Vic Devlin's hulk was suddenly on his back.

Farrell reacted immediately, bending and flipping
the outlaw over his head. Passengers on the aisle leapt
toward the windows to escape Devlin's flying feet. Stuart was coming at Farrell again, but Devlin's hurling
bulk hit him and knocked him down.

The husky Devlin was almost immediately up, and
began swinging the dangling open handcuff at the marshal. Farrell ducked it, but the cuff caught his hat and
sent it sailing. Planting his feet as best he could in the
rocking coach, he sent a fist to Devlin's jaw, thrusting
the outlaw backward—once again into Mel Stuart. Both
of them went down in a heap, with Devlin on top,
groggy from the blow.

Tug Farrell ran to him, intending to shackle Devlin
to one of the seat legs bolted to the floor, then subdue
Stuart. But when he hauled Devlin over to the closest
metal leg, Stuart was able to scramble to his feet and
run toward the rear of the car.

Cursing, Farrell quickly snapped the handcuff
around the leg, testing it to make sure it was secure.
Then he sprinted down the aisle after Stuart. He pulled
open the door to the platform and looked through into
the fourth car to see the outlaw running toward the
rear. Stuart collided with the conductor, then shoved
the railroad man out of his way and kept running. Farrell raced into the car.

"Hey!" shouted the conductor. "What's going on
here?"

Farrell flashed his badge.

"You're a lawman?"

"Yes! U.S. marshal!"

Annoyed at losing precious moments, Tug Farrell
hurried after Stuart, who was bolting through the doorway, leaving in his wake dozens of gaping passengers.

Farrell got out to the platform in time to see Stuart climbing the ladder leading to the top of the car, and he instantly followed. Stuart reached the roof of the coach, then sat down and braced himself, kicking at the marshal with his right foot as Farrell came within range. The lawman saw the boot coming and ducked in time to avoid it, but when he raised up, the outlaw lashed out again, and the heel of his boot connected with Farrell's left cheekbone. The blow snapped his head back, and he slipped down the ladder slightly before catching himself. He shook his head, and blood sprayed from the gash on his cheek. Then, bracing himself, he started climbing again.

His eyes wild, Stuart was waiting, and he swung his foot violently. Farrell dodged it, and this time he was fast enough to grasp the boot at the instep. Stuart swore, struggling to pull free. Suddenly he wrenched his foot out of the boot, leaving it in the marshal's hand.

The outlaw stood up on top of the rocking car and headed toward the front of the train, thrown off balance by the loss of his boot. Letting the boot drop, Farrell climbed onto the roof and pursued his quarry.

While the marshal scurried after him, Stuart paused as he reached the front end of the car, studying the gap between himself and car number three. He whipped his head around to see how close the lawman was behind him. Farrell was about ten feet away, shouting, "You've got nowhere to go, Stuart! Give it up!"

The desperate outlaw turned, squatted to get leverage, and leapt onto the roof of the next car. Landing awkwardly, with his right ankle twisted, he howled and slipped, his legs dangling off the edge of the car.

Farrell assessed Stuart's predicament. Then he sprang for the platform of car number three, reaching as he did so for the outlaw's coat and using his weight to drag Stuart over the edge. The two of them fell onto the platform, with the outlaw smashing his chin against the railing. But Stuart recovered and stood up and began swinging his fists wildly. Fighting with the desperation of a cornered tiger, the outlaw repelled all the lawman's attempts to subdue him.

But finally Tug Farrell's advantage in size and strength won out. He landed a solid punch on the outlaw's jaw, and Stuart stumbled, falling onto the railing. Leaning over, the marshal reached down and seized Stuart's coattail. Then he shouted to make himself heard, "We're going inside, Stuart! You and Devlin are both under arrest!"

"Okay! Okay!" Stuart shouted back, gripping the railing. "Let go of me!"

Farrell complied, but when he did, Stuart twisted around and leapt at the marshal in an attempt to push him backward off the platform. However, the seasoned lawman second-guessed Stuart and side-stepped the blow, and the outlaw sailed past him, sliding across the platform and ending up with his feet dangling over the side. He screamed in terror, struggling for a handhold when the train rounded a curve and the coach lurched sideways.

Farrell went to his aid, grabbing for the outlaw's hand. He caught hold of his fingers, but before he could pull him to safety, Stuart started slipping from his grip.

"Please!" the man screeched. His legs flapped dangerously close to the wheels.

Farrell braced himself and pulled harder, but Stuart's strength gave out and his fingers slid from the lawman's hold and he slipped beneath the train. His horrified wailing lasted only a moment before he was crushed to death by the whirring wheels.

Leaning over the platform railing, the marshal looked back on the tracks, visible because of the long curve. Mel Stuart's grotesquely tangled body was a bloody heap between the silver tracks.

The conductor rushed onto the platform, ordering the curious onlookers who were gathered by the doors to stay in their cars. Farrell showed the trainman his badge, then pinned it back on while explaining his mission. The conductor looked at Farrell's bloody face and gestured toward the third car. "Marshal, I'd suggest you make use of the washroom in the rear of this car. While you're cleaning yourself up a bit, I'll see that seats are rearranged so you can keep the other outlaw by your side."

"Thanks," Farrell responded, catching his breath. "I appreciate your help." Stepping into the car, he went directly into the washroom and looked at his face in the mirror. Grimacing, he murmured, "I'd frighten a blind man." Aside from the ugly gash on his cheekbone, there were a cut and a long purple mark where the handcuff had struck his forehead. The blood was dried on his forehead and had almost quit running from his cheek— but not before smearing his face, shirt, and coat.

He worked the pump, and water poured into the basin. Soaking a towel, he then pressed it against his face, and the coolness revived him somewhat. He then gingerly washed the dried blood from his face, although there was nothing he could do about his clothing. Moments later, Farrell emerged from the washroom and slowly walked up the aisle toward his prisoner, who was still handcuffed to the chair. A young man handed the lawman his hat, and Farrell thanked him while putting it on. After carefully placing Devlin's revolver in his own suitcase, the lawman got the conductor to help him with his prisoner. Moments later the outlaw was seated by the window and the U.S. marshal had the aisle seat, the two of them handcuffed to each other.

Devlin immediately turned to Farrell and asked, "What happened to Mel?"

The marshal gave him a bland look and replied, "Let's just say your pal won't have to worry about facing a trial. But you will, after we return from a side trip to Sacramento. You see, I'm picking up two more outlaws who are wanted in Colorado. All three of you will be going back to Denver with me—and all of you will stand trial for murder."

# Chapter Eight

The Union Pacific train rolled on toward California, periodically stopping at stations to take on or discharge passengers and freight or for water and coal. U.S. Marshal Tug Farrell soon realized it would be far safer—and far more comfortable—if his prisoner were shackled to the arm of his seat rather than to the lawman, so he used a spare pair of cuffs to do just that.

Vic Devlin remained quiet and sullen as the train chugged its way across Wyoming and then through Utah into the sunset. He refused to speak to his captor other than to notify him that he had to use the toilet at the rear of the car. It was only at such times that Farrell cautiously released the outlaw from the seat and handcuffed Devlin's wrist to his own so the lawman could accompany him. Then came the moment he worried about the most: Since the toilet was quite small, Farrell had to unshackle the outlaw from him and handcuff Devlin's hands together in front of him and allow Devlin to enter the toilet alone. So far Vic Devlin had not tried to escape. So far. . . .

Night fell. Boxed meals were handed out by the conductor, and soon the passengers were making ready to sleep while the train continued to carry them westward.

At midmorning the next day, the train rounded the northern tip of the Great Salt Lake and rolled into Promontory Point, Utah. While the engine was being serviced, the passengers and crew were fed a hot meal in a mess hall provided by the railroad. After eating, they were allowed a half-hour to walk around before reboarding.

Handcuffed together, Tug Farrell and Vic Devlin strolled near the massive engine and watched it take on water. Word had spread through the train of the outlaw's being captured by the federal marshal, although most of the passengers had not seen the two together, and the time allowed for them to stretch their legs now gave the passengers an opportunity to observe the two men up close. The children were especially interested, and some of the boys were bold enough to walk right up to the pair and stare.

One tousle-headed youth of about twelve studied the metal link between them, then spoke up in a forthright manner. "Hey, Marshal, that man looks pretty tough. Where you takin' him?"

"Sacramento," came Farrell's reply.

The boy looked hard at Devlin, then spoke to Farrell again. "What if he tries to get away from you, Marshal? I mean, what if he tries to get your gun and kill you?"

Looking down at his prisoner, some four inches shorter than he was, although about the same weight, Farrell glared at the outlaw while he answered the boy. "If he tries it, son, he'll be mighty sorry. *Mighty* sorry."

After a few more minutes, it was time to get back on the train. The pair entered the coach, and as they sat down in their seats the big marshal remarked, "I'm sure you entertained such thoughts before the kid made his suggestion. But just remember and be warned: I owe you for my dad, so don't push your luck."

Devlin pressed his lips tight in a grim line and his eyes showed the lawman the hostility he felt toward him. Without uttering a word, he turned and stared out the window.

The train pulled out of Promontory Point and angled southwest toward the Nevada border. Just after sundown, it pulled into a station to be serviced again, and Tug Farrell took his sullen prisoner for a brief walk.

As they strolled on the depot platform at the edge of the
tiny town that was no more than a speck on the face of
the barren Nevada desert, the lawman noticed a
strange look in Vic Devlin's eyes, and he was sure the
man was flirting with the idea of attempting an escape.
Farrell found himself almost wishing the bloody murderer would try it. But either Devlin thought better of
the idea or decided to bide his time, for he tried nothing
and they reboarded the train uneventfully.

At sunrise on the third day, the conductor moved
through the cars shouting, "Reno, twenty minutes!
Reno, Nevada, twenty minutes!"

Tug Farrell wakened and stretched his cramped
body. Pulling out a train schedule from his pocket, he
saw that there would be a lengthy stop in Reno to service the engine for the long, strenuous haul over the
high Sierra range. That would give him time to find the
telegraph office and send a wire to Sheriff Bob Sovern,
advising him that he was indeed on his way and would
be in Sacramento the next day.

The conductor had just disappeared from the car
when Vic Devlin turned to Farrell and grunted, "I gotta
go to the privy."

"You can wait till we get to Reno," Farrell replied
flatly. "You heard the man. It's only twenty minutes."

"But I can't wait that long," insisted the outlaw.

Farrell grumbled, but stood up. Unlocking the outlaw from the seat, the marshal escorted his prisoner
toward the rear of the coach. When the pair reached
the rear of the car, they found the toilet was occupied.
Devlin carried on, saying he was in dire need and cursing whoever was behind the door. Presently the door
opened, revealing the fat woman who had sat beside
Mel Stuart. As she stepped out, she looked up at the two
men, then scowled at Devlin.

Devlin glared back at her, mumbling, "About
time."

From a vest pocket, the marshal produced a small
key and unlocked the cuff on his right wrist. Then, just

as the lawman was slipping off the cuff, Devlin grabbed for Farrell's gun. But the seasoned lawman's instincts were well-honed and, sensing the move a fraction of a second before it came, he swiveled his hip so that when Devlin clawed for the gun, his hand closed on nothing but air. At the same time, Farrell slammed the outlaw on the nose with his elbow. Devlin's eyes watered from the pain, but he was desperate, and he punched Farrell in the belly and made another attempt to seize the holstered gun.

This time, Devlin's fingers closed on the butt of the revolver, but the marshal knocked Devlin's hand away. Swearing loudly, the outlaw threw a punch at Farrell's jaw, but the marshal ducked, and Devlin's fist cracked hard against the wall of the coach. Howling, he lashed out again, attempting to overpower Farrell.

Tug Farrell went blind with rage. Dodging the outlaw's strong hands, he gripped his shoulder and spun him around so that he faced the rear door of the coach. He clamped the back of Devlin's neck and rammed his face into the window, shattering the glass. Devlin pushed against the strong hands that held him, but Farrell's strength was too great and he drove the outlaw into what was left of the window again. One of the shards of glass pierced the outlaw's left eye, and he screamed in agony.

The outlaw fell to the floor, plucking wildly at the sliver of glass that protruded from his eyeball, but his hand was shaking so severely, he could not grasp it. Farrell leaned down and swatted Devlin's hand aside, saying, "Hold still, and let me get it."

Quickly the marshal removed the piece of glass. The horrified outlaw blinked against the blood that flowed from his eye and wailed, "I can't see out of my eye! You blinded my eye, Farrell!"

While Vic Devlin swore and railed at Farrell, the marshal sent someone to find the conductor and tell him what had happened. The trainman appeared, holding a wet towel, and the outlaw was taken back to his seat with the towel pressed against his face. Farrell shackled the man's hands together, telling him to keep his head back to relieve the pressure on the eye.

Seething with fury, the outlaw told the lawman, "You blinded me, Farrell . . . and I swear I'll get you for this!"

"Listen, Devlin," Farrell snapped, "you jumped me, remember? If you hadn't tried to escape, you'd still have your sight in that eye. Blame yourself, mister, not me!" He glared at his prisoner, then growled, "Besides, when you climb onto the gallows, you might prefer not being able to see at all."

Devlin's body stiffened, but he said nothing.

Moments later, the train began slowing down as it approached Reno. When the conductor came through the car, Farrell stopped him and asked, "How long is the stop in Reno?"

"Forty-five minutes."

"I need to get this man to a doctor, but we must be on the train when it leaves. Can you hold it up for me if we're not back by the time you're supposed to pull out?"

The portly conductor rubbed his jaw and said, "Well, seeing as how you're a U.S. marshal and you're on government business, I can hold the train for an additional half hour. But I don't think I can hold it beyond that."

"I'll be back as quick as I can," Farrell assured him. "Let me make it clear to you, though, that we *must* be on the train when it pulls out."

"Yes, sir," the conductor responded. "Just hurry, will you?"

Ominous black clouds hung over the towering Sierras as the train rolled westward out of Reno, Nevada, twenty minutes behind schedule. U.S. Marshal Tug Farrell sat beside his prisoner, who now sported a large bandage on his left eye held in place by an inch-wide strip of gauze wrapped around his head several times. With all the time taken up by the visit to the doctor—who had verified that Devlin's sight in his left eye was gone—Tug Farrell had not been able to send a wire to Sheriff Bob Sovern.

The train was just beginning to climb into the Sierras when rain began to spatter on the windows of the coach. Soon water was running over the windows in a steady sheet, and although it was still early morning, it looked almost as dark as night. The huge engine chugged and belched smoke in thick black billows as it strained to pull its five heavily loaded cars up the steep, winding grade in the face of the raging storm.

Tug Farrell looked over at his prisoner. Vic Devlin had been given medicinal powders by the doctor to ease his pain, and he was sleeping fitfully, oblivious of the storm raging outside. The marshal felt no remorse for Devlin's suffering—in fact, he had to admit that he felt it was justifiable retribution and wished a whole lot more suffering on the cold-blooded killer.

Lightning crackled repeatedly, illuminating the car with brief flares of blue-white light, although the noise the train made obscured the sound of the thunder. Farrell glanced out the window, thinking that the weather was as dramatic as the scenery—what he could see of it.

The storm lashed the train for the rest of the day and all that night. When morning came, the rain was still coming in torrents, and the mountain winds whipped it violently through the rugged canyons. Vic Devlin had given his captor no further trouble, although Tug Farrell was sure that the outlaw was raging as much as the storm. He was just not showing it.

As had become their custom, as soon as both of them were awake, Farrell took Devlin to the rear of the car to the toilet. After using the facilities, the lawman and his prisoner returned to their seats. Farrell was about to unlock Devlin from his own wrist and shackle him to the seat when the train abruptly made a wrenching jerk, and the lawman and his prisoner were slammed against the seats in front of them. Over the sound of the wind came the squealing of steel on steel as the brakes were hurriedly applied.

Those passengers who had not been thrown against the seats were tossed into the aisles as the brakes were applied. Men, women, and children screamed in terror as luggage came raining down from the overhead racks, smashing onto them. Managing to pick his way through the melee was the conductor, who shouted repeatedly, "Washout up ahead! Washout up ahead! Brace yourselves if you can!" as he made his way through the car to the next one.

Up ahead in the locomotive, the engineer could only watch helplessly as the engine slid inexorably down the steep mountain toward the gaping hole in the track a dozen yards away, taking with it five cars filled with travelers headed for certain disaster. With a sudden lurch, the engine hit the span of unsupported track and broke through, plowing down into mud. The six cars crumpled against one another, jackknifed, and keeled into the vast chasm, tumbling and breaking apart and scattering debris and bodies as they plummeted two hundred feet to the canyon floor.

At the bottom of the canyon, about a quarter-mile from where the engine and cars thundered down, was a small settlement of hunters and trappers and their families. At the arresting sound of the squealing brakes moments earlier, the people had bolted from their tents and cabins into the driving rain, fearing the worst. Wide-eyed, they looked over at the gorge in time to see the horrific sight of the cars breaking up like matchboxes.

The settlers immediately rallied, slogging through the mud to the crash site. Bending their heads into the driving rain, the men and women reached the site within ten minutes, pausing to look in horror at the broken and twisted wreckage that minutes earlier had been the temporary home of hundreds of people. As they made their way through the dozens of smashed trees, the settlers noted the engine lying on its side and hissing as plumes of steam rose from deep in its steel bowels.

The rescuers barely knew where to begin in the carnage. Bodies were strewn everywhere, some moving but others still. Frequently what had at first appeared to be twisted hunks of metal and broken slabs of wood were in fact twisted, broken bodies of men, women, and children. Some of the lifeless forms hung from shattered windows, including the engineer's, whose bloody body was draped over the side of the cab, halfway out the engine's window. The rain was washing his blood away. The wails and moans of the surviving passengers filled the canyon, from those who had been thrown clear of the wreck and from those trapped inside the crumpled cars.

The rescuers pulled themselves from their shock and began dashing to those people they could tell were still alive. One of the men heard a child crying somewhere near, and squinting through the rain, his eyes searched the wreckage. Suddenly he saw something amid the debris near one of the cars—a small body clad in a frilly dress. He ran toward it, dodging hunks of metal, boulders, and obviously dead bodies. Reaching the muddied form, he bent down, praying as he did so. He turned it over and found big round eyes staring at him from a porcelain head. One side of the doll's face was crushed, making its painted smile seem like a mockery. Shuddering, the man stood up and listened. The crying had stopped.

Inside the third coach, which lay on its side against the car that had been behind it, Vic Devlin slowly became aware of the wails and cries around him. There was severe pain in his left eye, and water was dripping in his face. At first he thought he was in the midst of a nightmare, but then he started recalling what had happened, vaguely recollecting being flung about inside the railroad car.

Devlin opened his right eye and realized that he was lying on his back. Directly above him was a broken window through which the cold, steady rain was falling, pelting him in the face. Why did his left eye hurt so bad? Raising his hand to it, he felt the bandage—and saw the shackle. Everything came rushing back.

*That's right,* he thought to himself. *Me and Farrell had just gotten back to our seats when the train lurched and somebody shouted somethin' about a washout. I guess I must've been knocked out—and I guess we've been wrecked.* Devlin turned his head. U.S. Marshal Tug Farrell was lying beside him with his eyes closed. Devlin's heart started beating faster. *Maybe he's dead!* he thought gleefully, but then he saw the slow rise and fall of his chest. "Terrific," he muttered. "I'm handcuffed to a knocked-out lawman."

Then it was as if a light came on inside the outlaw's brain. Farrell was out cold! This was Devlin's chance to escape! All he had to do was find the key to the handcuffs. One little twist of the wrist, and Vic Devlin was a free man! He sat up and began searching for the key in Farrell's vest pockets, when he heard loud, excited voices above the wails and cries of the injured passengers around him. The outlaw knew immediately that people were coming to the rescue—which meant he had to get away quick. Frantically he fished for the key, but it was not to be found in the vest.

Devlin looked quickly around. No one was paying any attention to him. Working fast, the outlaw climbed over the seats, dragging the heavy, inert body of Tug Farrell to the end of the car and climbing outside into the rain. There were a couple of men helping some injured a few yards away, and several others were drawing near. Moving as fast as he could, Devlin dragged Farrell away from the coach and finally laid him down behind a dense clump of shrubbery.

With trembling fingers he fumbled furiously through all of the marshal's pockets for the key. It was nowhere to be found. Where was it? Farrell had always kept it in one of the vest pockets before. Why wasn't it there now? Cursing under his breath, Devlin suddenly realized it must have fallen out after the crash.

The outlaw's head snapped up as he heard voices

nearby. The rescuers were scurrying about in search of all who might have been thrown from the cars. If Devlin tried to drag the unconscious lawman away from the bush, they would see him immediately. Deciding it was only a matter of time until they found him anyway, there was only one thing to do. . . .

Working as fast as he could with one free hand, he took Farrell's gun belt off and strapped it to his own waist, then pinned on the U.S. marshal's badge. Vic Devlin had barely finished arranging his masquerade when a woman spotted him sitting on the wet ground beside the limp form of Tug Farrell. She called over her shoulder for assistance, and then hurried to Devlin's side.

As she drew up, Devlin blinked against the rain in his face and said, "Howdy, ma'am."

Eyeing the badge, the woman responded, "Hello, Marshal." She gestured with her thumb and explained, "We're all from a nearby settlement. It's a lucky thing for you people that this accident happened where it did; otherwise, nobody might've found you for days. Are you hurt bad, Marshal?"

"No, ma'am," Devlin replied with a slight smile. "My legs are givin' me some pain, but nothin' real bad. My, uh, prisoner, here, is out cold, though. We really did some tumblin' around inside the coach when it went off the tracks and over the cliff. He seems to have a nasty bruise on his head." Holding out his free hand, he added, "Oh, by the way, my name's Tug Farrell. U.S. Marshal Tug Farrell."

At that moment, a big husky man joined them, and the woman advised him, "Jake, this man's a U.S. marshal, and the prisoner shackled to him is alive but unconscious." Then to Devlin she said, "This is my husband, Jake Greenwalt, Marshal. I'm Elizabeth Greenwalt."

"Where you from, Marshal?" Jake Greenwalt asked.

"I work out of the Denver office."

"And who might your prisoner be?"

"Name's Vic Devlin," replied the impersonator.

"Vic Devlin? I think I've heard of him."

"Oh?" said Devlin, feeling a warm flow of satisfaction run through him.

"Bad dude."

"Yeah. That he is."

Making up his lies quickly, Devlin told the pair that while capturing the outlaw, he had been injured in the eye. Wanting to be free of Farrell, he explained that the key to the handcuffs had evidently fallen from his pocket in the crash. "Can one of you people go fetch some kind of tool from your village that can remove the cuffs? It'd be easier to carry my prisoner back there for medical attention if we're separated."

Jake Greenwalt, however, shook his head. "Since you're not badly hurt, you can walk while we carry the outlaw. That'd save time. If you still want the cuffs removed when we get there, we'll cut them off with a hacksaw or something."

Devlin kept his anger to himself. He did not like the delay in being freed from Farrell, but he felt it best not to protest. They might start to wonder why he was so anxious to be separated from the man he was supposed to be guarding.

By the time they reached the settlement, Tug Farrell was starting to regain consciousness. The big lawman opened his eyes, blinked, and tried to sit up, but then he put his hand to his head and lay back down. When he opened his eyes again, a woman was hovering over him.

"You must lie still, Mr. Devlin," she said. "You got a real nasty bump on your head, and you've been unconscious."

Farrell screwed up his face. Something the woman had just said rankled him—but already he could not remember what it was. His head was throbbing, and he was horribly dizzy. Slowly it came back to him that the train had hit a washout and— Vic Devlin! Where was he? Farrell glanced over and a wave of relief washed over him. He was still shackled to the brutal outlaw, who was regarding him with aversion.

Suddenly Farrell saw the badge on the outlaw's chest. He raised up with a start and demanded, "Hey! What're you doing with—"

"Mr. Devlin!" cut in Elizabeth Greenwalt. "Please lie down."

Then it hit Farrell. What had rankled him was the woman calling him Mr. Devlin. He looked at the badge again, then slapped his hand to his side. In the same instant, he saw his gun on the outlaw's hip and a wicked sneer curling Devlin's mouth.

The outlaw turned to a large, muscular man hovering closely and said, "Okay, Mr. Greenwalt. I'd appreciate it if you cut these cuffs off now."

Farrell looked from Devlin to Greenwalt. "No, wait! You can't let this man go! He's a cold-blooded murderer, and you can't let him get away!"

Devlin grinned maliciously. "Why, Vic Devlin," he said dryly, "you behave yourself or I'll tell these nice folks not to feed you before they lock you up for the night in the shed out back."

"What?" Farrell shouted.

"Sure," Devlin said. "I need a good night's sleep after that awful wreck, and the only way I'm gonna get one is if I don't have to worry about you tryin' to escape. Since I lost the key to these cuffs during the crash, Mr. Greenwalt's offered to cut 'em off for me. We'll hold you out back till we can travel tomorrow. These kindly folks have told me there's a stagecoach comes through here twice a week, headed for Sacramento. I'll make sure you're tied up good and tight, and we'll catch it in the mornin'."

The lawman gritted his teeth. "That's quite a convincing tale, Devlin. Only I'm sure that by morning you'll be long gone." He glared at Devlin's repugnant face, then asked, "How come you didn't kill me while you had the chance? I'm sure you wanted to." The lawman then sniffed derisively and exclaimed, "Oh, of course! It wouldn't have looked too good for a lawman to gun down the man he's shackled to."

For just an instant Vic Devlin's eyes betrayed him. Then he recovered himself and blithely shook his head. "Nice try, Devlin. If I didn't know better, I'd almost be convinced by you myself. Guess what it comes down to is it's my word against yours—and the fact that this badge is pinned to my chest, not yours."

Tug Farrell had had enough of Vic Devlin's trickery, and of his insolence. Without warning, he punched the outlaw savagely in the jaw, stunning him, then made a lunge for the revolver holstered around his waist.

"Hold it right there!" Jake Greenwalt bellowed. Grabbing a rifle from beside the door, he lined the barrel on Farrell, jacking a cartridge into the chamber.

Farrell stayed his hand. Panting from the exertion, he explained, "Look, mister, the truth is, I am U.S. Marshal Tug Farrell, not him."

Elizabeth Greenwalt stepped beside her husband, worry in her eyes. "Jake, do you think he's telling the truth?"

Her husband chuckled humorlessly and replied, "He's just desperate, woman." Eyeing Farrell, he ordered, "Now, you just put your hand as high in the air as you can—and as far away from that revolver as possible."

Farrell obeyed, glancing down at his semiconscious adversary.

"Liz," said Jake, "you take the rifle and keep it pointed straight at him while I go over there and get the marshal's gun out of the holster."

When Greenwalt stepped close, Farrell told him, "I can prove to you that I'm the lawman and he's the outlaw."

The settler eyed him suspiciously. "I'm listening."

"You don't need to cut the cuffs off 'cause I've got a spare. There's a tiny pocket on the inside of that gun belt. Go ahead. Check it for yourself."

The big hunter gave Farrell a look of surprise, then

unhooked the gun belt from Devlin's waist and searched it. While Farrell kept his right hand extended toward the ceiling, Jake Greenwalt found the key. He looked back at Farrell, his eyes wide.

"Now reach into my shirt pocket. The one on the right," Farrell instructed.

Watching the big muscular man carefully, the settler reached into the designated pocket and produced a damp, folded piece of paper. Opening it, he saw that it was a wanted poster of Vic Devlin. Jake looked from the poster to the outlaw and back again. Then he raised his eyes to Tug Farrell's face.

"I'm sorry, mister," the settler mumbled.

"It's okay," Farrell replied with a grin. "If I didn't know who I was, I might've believed him, too."

# Chapter Nine

The sun was midway through the morning sky when the stagecoach turned onto Sacramento's main street and rolled to a stop in front of the county jail. U.S. Marshal Tug Farrell climbed down, dragging his prisoner with him, then thanked the driver for saving him the walk from the Pacific Overland Stagelines office, two blocks away.

Sheriff Bob Sovern was talking with his two deputies when Farrell and Devlin entered the office. The U.S. marshal paused just inside the doorway and addressed the man behind the desk. "Sheriff Sovern? I'm Tug Farrell. You have a spare cell? I've got a fella here who needs one."

Sovern was on his feet instantly, extending his hand to the marshal. Looking the bruised, battered, and bandaged outlaw and lawman over, he commented, "You two get that way fighting each other or some common enemy?"

"A little of both," Farrell replied, grinning. "It's a long story. The train we were on took a nasty spill over the side of a cliff. We just came in on the stage."

Sovern introduced Farrell to John Way and Ed Willis. Then he said to the marshal, "Who's this you're cuffed to?"

"Vic Devlin. Ever hear of him?"

"Can't say that I have," responded Sovern. "What're you going to do with him?"

"Well, he *was* planning on settling down in your

fair state, but the U.S. government has other ideas—like
trying him for bank robbery and murder. I'll be escort-
ing him back to Denver along with Raven Morrow and
Clete Hobbs, if that's who your two prisoners are. You
*do* still have them behind bars, don't you?"

"Sure do," Sovern assured him. "We'll stick your
friend here in the cell next to the fella calling himself
Clarence Hoffman. You can take a look at him right
now."

Deputies Way and Willis tagged along as the sheriff
led Farrell and Devlin to the men's cells. Four other
men besides Clete Hobbs were presently incarcerated
—although their crimes were nothing worse than
drunk-and-disorderly. Hobbs lay on his bunk with his
hat over his face, masking him. His cellmate, along with
all the other prisoners, stared curiously as Sovern
opened the empty cell next to the one that held Hobbs.
Farrell walked Devlin into the ten-by-ten cubicle, then
unlocked the handcuffs that bound the two of them
together. Rubbing his chafed wrist, the outlaw gave
Farrell a murderous look, then sat down on the bunk.

Farrell said, "Don't get too comfortable, Devlin.
You won't be here long. Just a couple of days, and then
the four of us will be on our way back to Denver."

Devlin grunted. "You're gonna have fun tryin' to
get three of us *anywhere,* lawman."

Ignoring the remark, the marshal stepped out of
the cell and examined the faces in the other cubicles
while Sovern closed and locked the door. He turned to
the sheriff and, his face reflecting his keen disappointment, muttered, "I don't see him. Which one is Hoffman?"

Clete Hobbs's cellmate was standing at the door,
blocking the cot from view. "That one," replied Sovern,
gesturing to the man at the rear of the adjoining cell. He
motioned for the man at the barred door to move, then
called, "Hey, Hobbs! You got company!"

The man on the bunk stirred, lifted the hat from his
face, and swore as he sat up. His eyes were bleary and
his face was groggy as he snapped, "I told you, Sheriff,

my name ain't—" His tongue froze when he locked eyes with the marshal.

Farrell was clearly relieved. Smiling triumphantly, he declared, "'Morning, Hobbs. Nice to see you again. Seen Raven lately? No matter. You'll be seeing a lot of each other during the next few days—on our trip back to Denver."

Hatred flared in Clete Hobbs's eyes. Sneering, he retorted crisply, "You'll never get me and Raven back to Colorado, Farrell!"

Moving closer to the bars, Tug Farrell shook his head slowly. "You must have learned your threats from Devlin, here," he mocked. Then his face hardened and he glared at Hobbs with piercing eyes. "Not only will I get you to Colorado, but I'll watch you take the plunge to the end of a rope. Both of you!"

Hobbs stared intently at the U.S. marshal for a long moment. Then he silently lay back down on his bunk.

Farrell said to Sovern, "I want to see Raven."

When the lawmen had passed from the cellblock, Vic Devlin moved to the bars that separated him from Hobbs's cell. Peering through the bars, he asked, "Hey, what's between you and the tin star?"

Clete Hobbs sat up and spewed out his story along with his hatred for Tug Farrell. When Hobbs had finished, Devlin gripped the bars until his knuckles turned white. "You got good reason to hate the man's guts, all right," the outlaw said. "Nearly as good as mine. I'm wearin' this bandage 'cause Farrell blinded me—and let me tell you, I'm gonna get revenge for it. Sweet revenge. I'm gonna kill him if it's the last thing I do."

As Tug Farrell and Bob Sovern headed through the cellblock to the women's side of the jail, the marshal could see Raven Morrow smoking a cigarillo and chatting with Maude Esther Dodd through the bars that separated them. The prisoners' conversation immediately broke off when they heard the approaching footsteps, and the women looked the lawmen's way as the pair came into view. When Raven saw Farrell, her face went chalky white and the cigarillo fell from her mouth. Recovering, she quickly bent down and retrieved the smoking butt, pausing briefly before she stood up to face the man whose heart she had shattered three years before.

Farrell thought that she was working hard—but not quite succeeding—at regaining her composure, and she regarded him indifferently for a moment, then looked at the sheriff.

Sheriff Bob Sovern said tauntingly, "Still insist that your name is Rita Marston, lady?"

Shrugging, the beautiful brunette replied tonelessly, "You knew it wasn't, anyhow."

Tug Farrell felt his heart skip a beat as he beheld the fascinating woman who had so easily captured his heart. He had once loved her deeply—and she had gone so far in her masquerade as a rancher's daughter to accept his proposal of marriage. On that awful day when he learned her true identity, he had been stunned and heartbroken . . . and in her cruelty she had laughed in his face, mocking him for being such a blind fool. She shifted her gaze from the sheriff to the marshal, and as their eyes met and locked, Farrell's heart settled back to normal. All he felt for her now was disgust.

Moving to the bars, Raven brushed her long hair back from her face and asked, "So you're planning on taking Clete and me back to Denver to hang, eh, Farrell?"

"Yep," he responded without emotion. "It'll sort of be like hanging a couple of ghosts."

She smiled at him coldly. "Fooled you for a while, didn't we?"

"Until a few days ago."

"I guess you're pretty sure you'll get extradition."

"Yep."

"How'd you find out we were here?"

"I'll tell you all about it on the trip back. Won't be long before we'll be traveling. I'm going to see the governor tomorrow morning—so I'd say you should be prepared for a journey the day after."

At ten o'clock the next morning, U.S. Marshal Tug Farrell was admitted to the governor's office, where he presented his case against Raven Morrow and Clete Hobbs. California's chief executive agreed to extradite the two murderers, promising he would have the papers drawn up and ready the next day. While the governor talked to an aide about the necessary procedures, Farrell decided that when he left the governor's office he would go to the train depot. There he would reserve a compartment for his three prisoners and himself, deciding it would be far easier to keep them secure—and keep a watchful eye on them—if they were taken back to Denver in confined quarters. He would also check to see if they needed to take the southern route through Bakersfield, then head east for Denver, or whether the tracks in the Sierras had been repaired and that route was reopened.

While Tug Farrell was at the governor's office, Sheriff Bob Sovern discussed a minor problem at a nearby ranch with his two deputies. The sheriff decided that Ed Willis could handle the matter by himself, and he sent him out of town. Sitting behind his desk, Sovern flipped through the stack of mail that waited for attention and sighed. Then, looking up at John Way, he told the young deputy, "You go ahead and patrol the street for a while. Keep the town quiet so I can concentrate on this mail."

"Will do," the deputy replied, grinning.

Way turned to head for the door, but as he did so, the rough-and-rugged bulk of Jack Bullard stormed in, holding a cocked revolver. Bullard was followed close behind by Mack Dugan, Earl Penrod, and six new gang members—all with weapons drawn. The last man to enter closed the door behind him.

Both lawmen tensed but did not make a move for their guns. Facing nine men with revolvers in their hands, the sheriff and deputy knew better than to try to make a fight of it.

While Way stood as still as a statue, except for his eyes roving over the hard faces of the intruders, Sovern stood up and asked, "What do you want?"

"A couple of your prisoners, Sheriff," grunted the enormous outlaw, picking up a ring of keys from Sovern's desk. "Let's all of us go back to the jail."

After being disarmed, Sovern and Way were lined up shoulder to shoulder and forced to lead Bullard and his men into the cell area. Once they were out of the office—and out of sight of any passersby—Dugan and Penrod, each bearing a long-bladed knife, slipped up behind the lawmen. Before either Sovern or Way knew what was happening, the deadly blades were thrust into their backs to their hearts, and their lifeless bodies crumpled near the office door.

"Good work, fellas," Bullard praised his men. "Now, let's go get Raven and Clete."

Raven Morrow's eyes lit up when she saw Bullard and his men. "It's about time, Jack," she said, relief evident in her voice.

"I came for you as quick as I could," the huge man responded. "Took me a while to round me up some reinforcements. Glad to see me, huh?"

"More than I have time to tell you right now," she breathed. "What did you do with the sheriff and his deputies?"

Unlocking Raven's cell door, Bullard replied, "Only saw one deputy. He and the sheriff are both dead. You know how good Mack and Earl are with their knives."

The door creaked on its dry hinges when Jack Bullard pulled it open. As Raven hurried out, Maude Esther Dodd stepped to the bars of her cell and said in a low, pleading voice, "You're takin' me, right?"

Raven Morrow stopped and looked at the middle-aged buxom woman. "Sure." Glancing over her shoulder, she told Jack Bullard, "Let her out. She's going with us."

"Who is she?" queried Bullard while unlocking the door.

"A new friend of mine. Her name's Maude Esther Dodd—and she's okay. She wants to go to Canada with us. She'll do the cooking and the housework at the mine for a small cut of the gold. She's not asking for much . . . and she'll hang if we leave her here."

Two members of the county council made their way to the sheriff's office, discussing how Bob Sovern could help them with a particular problem that had arisen. When Joshua Turner and Hal Frame entered the office, they found it unoccupied.

Frame suggested, "Let's check the jail. He's probably back there."

The two men crossed the room and pushed open the door that led to the cell area, unprepared for the sight that greeted them: Bob Sovern and John Way lay dead on the floor in pools of blood. The councilmen gasped and stared first at the corpses, then at each other, mouths gaping. At the same time, they heard the creak of a cell door swinging open and voices coming from the same direction.

Turner whispered, "Somebody's breaking prisoners out of the jail!"

Nodding, Frame whispered in return, "I'll bet it's that bunch of rough-looking scabs we saw ride into town a few minutes ago. The ones who left their horses down by the feed store!"

"Let's go!" the banker whispered urgently, heading for the door. "We've got to get help quick!"

Clete Hobbs smiled from ear to ear as his cell was unlocked. "Am I glad to see you!" he told Jack Bullard. Looking at Raven, who stood beside the huge outlaw, he said, "I was beginning to give up hope. With Farrell seeing the governor today, we're getting outta here by the skin of our teeth!"

Raven's dark eyes narrowed to wicked glints. *"Far-*

*rell!*" she spat, as if the name were poison. "He's going to get his!"

Smiling his agreement, Clete Hobbs hurried out of his cell.

From the adjoining cell, Vic Devlin spoke up. "Hobbs, unlock my door and let me out, will you?"

The rawboned outlaw turned and looked at the bank robber, as did Raven, who eyed Devlin's homely face and asked, "Who's he, Clete?"

"Farrell captured him on the train while coming here from Denver. Name's Devlin. Vic Devlin. He's all right. I'll let him out." As he spoke, Hobbs took the key ring from Jack Bullard's hand.

Laughing with demonic glee, Devlin told Raven, "Like you, lady, I got a grudge as big as a mountain against Farrell. Matter of fact, I'm gonna blow his guts all over California!"

Raven immediately stayed Clete Hobbs's hand from unlocking Devlin's cell. "Forget it, Clete," she said firmly, and started walking on.

Devlin's face went beet red with anger. "Whaddya mean, forget it? Didn't I impress you enough? Okay, how about if I rip Farrell limb from limb? Come on, lady! You gotta let me outta here!"

Raven stopped in her tracks and slowly turned toward the cell. Sneering at the desperate outlaw, she told him, "Oh, you impressed me, all right, Devlin, but the trouble is, if your grudge is that big, you'd just get in my way. You see, you aren't going to be the one to kill Farrell. That pleasure is going to be mine, and mine alone."

Devlin's foul oaths filled the cell area, and his expression was one of crazed fury.

Shouting to be heard over the outlaw, one of the other prisoners stood at his cell door and asked, "Hey, Clete, how about takin' us with you?"

Hobbs looked at the six new recruits, than queried Raven, "You want some more men?"

The brunette ran a disapproving gaze over the prisoners, whose sallow faces and watery eyes indicated that they were heavy drinkers. Shaking her head, she said, "Leave them. Drunken sots wouldn't last a half-day's ride. Come on, let's get out of here." With that, she strode toward the office with her men and Maude Esther following in her wake.

Vic Devlin gripped the bars. "Lady!" he screamed. "Don't leave me in here! Let me out!"

Raven kept walking. As she reached the end of the hallway, by the bodies of the lawmen, she yelled back over her shoulder, "You got yourself in there. Get yourself out."

The brunette then looked at Maude Esther and gestured at the bloody bodies. "Take the sheriff's gun belt. Clete and I will find ours out here in the office." With that, she stepped over the corpses and entered the office.

The Dodd woman bent over and unbuckled the gun belt from Bob Sovern's waist. She had a little problem getting it around her ample girth, but she finally succeeded in fastening the buckle in the last hole of the belt.

Raven and Hobbs found their gun belts and strapped them on while the other members of the gang took spare revolvers and ammunition. "Okay," Raven ordered, "we'll go out two at a time a few seconds apart. Clete and I will go first."

Jack Bullard suddenly pointed out, "Raven, we'll have to pick up a horse for the woman. We only brought two extras—one for you and one for Clete."

"No problem. We'll just grab one tied along the street."

Pulling the door open, Raven stepped outside, with Hobbs following her like an obedient dog. Suddenly a sharp voice cut the air from directly across the street. "Hold it right there! Every one of you throw down your guns and come out with your hands in the air!"

Raven stopped short and looked across. A number of men were partly visible hunkered behind barrels, wagons, and wooden crates along the boardwalk on the opposite side of the street. All of them had rifles and revolvers trained on the doorway of the sheriff's office.

"Everybody out!" shouted the same man, who was standing behind a wagon, holding a rifle. "Drop those guns *now*!"

Raven turned her head slightly and quietly asked Jack Bullard, "Where are the horses?"

"To your right. There by the feed store."

Nodding, she mused half-aloud, "About thirty yards." She paused, then half-whispered over her shoulder, "I can't tell how many men are drawing a bead on us, but it's now or never. Start shooting, and run for the horses. Maude Esther, grab one between here and there and get on it."

With that, Raven whipped out her revolver and sent a shot at the man who was giving orders. The bullet whizzed by his head, and he ducked behind the wagon.

The Morrow gang spilled out of the sheriff's office, guns blazing, and the street erupted with gunfire from both sides. The hail of lead from a dozen citizens forced the gang to dive for cover before they were halfway to their mounts. The battle intensified as the gang fired back from behind rain barrels, wagons, and buggies.

At the instant the firing began, a redheaded young mother and her son were rattling down the street in a wagon. The vehicle was caught in the unexpected cross fire, and both horses were hit. As the animals fell, screaming in agony, the horrified young mother acted quickly and flipped her redheaded, freckle-faced son into the bed of the wagon. Dropping down beside him, she pressed him flat against the floor, holding him close, as bullets flew overhead.

Firing from behind a rain barrel, Raven Morrow shot one of the townsmen, then called for her gang to start working their way toward the horses. The ten men and two women started darting along the boardwalk between places of cover, but first one and then another of their ranks fell under the hail of bullets. The battle was following the direction of the gang as they moved toward their horses.

More townsmen were joining the fight, and Raven knew they were going to have to surrender to avoid being wiped out unless they could get some kind of advantage. Reloading her revolver, she snapped the cylinder in place. As she looked across the street for a target, she suddenly focused on the mother and son in the wagon. A sly smile formed on her mouth and she turned to Jack Bullard, crouched ten feet away from her behind a large crate.

"Cover me, Jack!" she shouted. "I'm going to take control of this situation!"

The huge man looked at her questioningly, but said nothing. All of Raven's gang members learned very quickly that when she gave an order, it was wise to obey it.

Just before Raven darted out from behind the barrel, a third gang member took a bullet and fell. Cursing at the townsman's marksmanship, Raven gritted her teeth and dashed to the wagon while guns blazed over her head. Bullard kept up a steady barrage of bullets toward their adversaries across the way, making it hard for them to take aim at the beautiful brunette.

Holding her revolver in her right hand, Raven reached over the side of the wagon and sank her strong fingers into the back of the boy's shirt, pulling him up. "No!" the boy's mother shrieked, and clawed at the hand clutching her son.

Swearing, Raven brought the barrel down hard on the woman's temple, momentarily stunning her, and the boy screamed in terror.

When the redhead regained her senses, she looked up at the black-haired woman holding her son against her with the muzzle of the cocked revolver pressed to his head. Getting to her knees, she held out her hands, screaming, "Don't hurt him! Please, don't hurt him!"

The street fell quiet as the firing stopped. Smiling, Raven hollered, "That's better! If any one of you heroes tries anything, I'll blow this kid's head off!"

From behind the brunette came the laughter of her henchmen as they hurried toward their horses. "Good work, Raven," Clete Hobbs declared as he rushed by her.

Raven acknowledged his praise with a slight nod, then eyed the townsmen, standing as still as statues. "We're taking this kid with us," she told them. "And I'm warning you: If a posse follows us, they'll find this kid's carcass!"

"No, please!" begged the boy's mother, sobbing. "Don't take Tommy! If you have to have a hostage, take me!"

"Shut up!" snapped Raven. "If you want to see your kid again alive, you'd better make sure these people do as I say! If you follow my orders, I'll release him—in good time." She looked at the woman, then asked, "What's your name? I'll wire you, telling you where to find him when we're done needing him."

The woman choked back her sobs. "Millie Jordan."

Raven nodded. Carrying the boy under the arms, his feet dangling, she made her way toward the other gang members. "Get me my horse so we can hightail it out of here!" she commanded.

Jack Bullard quickly brought her mount to her. As she climbed into the saddle, settling Tommy Jordan in front of her, she looked at everyone along the street. "I repeat: No one make a move." Gesturing with her chin first at the bodies of four dead townsmen and then at two wounded men, she added, "Those good citizens don't care if they get to the undertakers' a few minutes later—and you two wounded gents are just going to have to wait for doctoring." She jabbed the gun against the boy's head for emphasis that she meant her threat. Then, spurring her horse, she led the gang out of Sacramento at a gallop. Over the sound of the retreating hoofbeats, Tommy's wails could be heard—growing fainter and fainter.

U.S. Marshal Tug Farrell arrived on the scene at a run, coming from the depot six blocks away. He had heard gunfire, but by the time he reached the main street, all he saw was a band of riders heading north out

of town in front of a cloud of dust. Racing to the place
they had left, he saw a crowd gathered around a hysterical, incoherent woman and bodies crumpled and
sprawled on the street.

Drawing close to the weeping woman, the lawman
said, "I'm United States Marshal Tug Farrell. What has
happened here?"

Answering for the redhead, a man explained excitedly, "There was a big jailbreak, Marshal! Outlaws
killed the sheriff and one of his deputies!"

The news hit Tug Farrell like a punch in the stomach. Whirling, he dashed to the sheriff's office and
plunged through the door. Hurrying across the office to
where several men were standing, he looked down and
saw the bodies of Bob Sovern and John Way. He pushed
past them, into the cell area, going to the women's
section first and finding it empty. Cursing angrily, he
ran to the men's cellblock, relieved to see that at least
Vic Devlin was still there.

Farrell turned and hurried back to the office. To the
men who were gathered there, he said, "Gentlemen,
I'm United States Marshal Tug Farrell. I came here to
extradite two of the prisoners your sheriff was holding
in the jail. Do you know where Deputy Willis is?"

"Don't know," spoke up an elderly man. "Maybe
he's outta town on an errand of some kind, seeing as
how he didn't come when all the shooting started."

"Did anyone see how many were in the gang?"
queried Farrell.

"I don't think anybody was able to stop and count
'em, Marshal," spoke up another man. "Tell you this
much, though: We killed three of 'em. But offhand I'd
say there were probably eight or nine that got away.
Two of 'em was women."

Wondering if one of the three who was killed might
be Clete Hobbs, Farrell went outside to examine the
bodies. Hobbs was not one of them.

Approaching the people gathered around the
weeping woman, the federal man explained to a man

on the fringe of the group that he had come to extradite Clete Hobbs and Raven Morrow to Colorado to stand trial for murder. "I've got to go after them," Farrell told them quickly. "Where is the nearest stable? I need to buy a horse."

"Oh, you can't do that, Marshal!" exclaimed one of the men. "They'll kill the boy."

"What boy? What are you talking about?"

Gesturing at the redheaded mother, the man explained, "The gang took Tommy Jordan with them—he's Millie's ten-year-old son. The woman that was in jail, she kidnapped him and said if a posse followed, she'd blow his head off."

"I'm not a posse," responded Farrell. "I'm one man."

Millie Jordan's wailing and sobbing was heartrending. Shaking his head, the man told Farrell, "If you go after them, it's going to make things even tougher on Millie, 'cause that black-haired woman said she'd turn Tommy loose in time if no one followed. Would you talk to her first, before you go?"

"Certainly," Farrell agreed. "Her name is Mrs. Jordan, you said?"

"That's right. Millie Jordan."

Farrell looked around, then asked, "Is her husband somewhere here in town?"

"No, sir. She's a widow. Tommy's all she's got."

Looking at the distraught woman, Tug Farrell swallowed hard and girded himself. He hoped that she would understand that he could not allow the outlaws to ride away without pursuit—although he admitted to himself that if he were in the woman's shoes, he doubted he would be understanding.

Farrell started toward the woman, when he saw Deputy Ed Willis trotting down the street. Bystanders on both sides of the street ran out to the deputy, converging around him like crows in a cornfield, to tell him what had happened. Willis's composure shattered as the details were quickly related to him.

"What are you men waiting for?" he finally shouted. "Get your horses and let's go after them!"

"We can't," one of the townsmen told him. "They took Tommy Jordan with them as a hostage, and they said they'll kill him if we go after them."

Willis spotted Tug Farrell, and he slid from his saddle and raced to the marshal's side, his expression one of incredulous disbelief. "You know these murderers, Farrell!" he blared. "Will they really kill Tommy Jordan if we pursue them? We can't just let that pack of wild animals ride away scot-free!"

Farrell sighed. "Raven Morrow is cold-blooded and vicious, and I assure you, she meant what she said. But don't worry. They're not going to get away, 'cause I'm going after them—alone."

"No!" a sharp voice suddenly commanded.

Farrell turned. Millie Jordan was staring at him, her eyes boring into him.

"Ma'am?" he asked.

"You are not to go after them! I won't have you endangering the life of my son!" There was fire in her blue eyes, and her face had all the ferocity of a mother bear protecting her cub.

Farrell stepped over to her. He could not help but notice that despite the woman's horrendous ordeal, she was remarkably self-possessed—and remarkably lovely. The sun danced in her copper-colored hair, and the plain gingham dress she wore did not hide the curves of her figure. The marshal guessed that she was around thirty-three, and he found himself wondering how long she had been widowed. He introduced himself, telling her, "I have to go after them, Mrs. Jordan. They've killed a lot of people, and they need to be stopped before they kill any more—including your son."

Her face paled. "My son?" she breathed, her hand going to her mouth. "But she promised . . ."

"Her promises mean nothing," Farrell countered, his words sharper than he had intended. "There's no assurance that she'd ever let him go. Raven Morrow's as unpredictable and deadly as a teased rattler. She's also heartless. If Tommy should do or say the wrong thing at the wrong time, she wouldn't bat an eye at killing him."

Millie Jordan began to tremble all over. "Wh-what can I do, Marshal Farrell?"

"It's what *I* can do, ma'am," he replied softly. "I'm an expert tracker, and I'll go after the gang alone—I must work alone to pursue them. I'll find a way to move in on them and rescue Tommy. Don't worry, I'll bring your boy back to you." He smiled down at her tenderly. "And that's a promise you can count on."

Farrell addressed Deputy Willis. "I need a good horse and a pack loaded with food, water, ammunition, and other supplies—including a small tent in case I run into bad weather."

Millie Jordan suddenly grabbed Farrell's arm. "Marshal, I'm going with you. I'm good on a horse, and I'll stay out of your way when you close in on them."

Shaking his head firmly, the marshal replied, "I can't let you do that, ma'am. Not only would it jeopardize my mission, but it would be too dangerous for you."

Millie persisted. "My son's only ten, and I want to be there when you get him away from them. He'll need me! I'm sure he's absolutely scared to death!"

Looking at her tenderly, the big man said, "Mrs. Jordan, I know this has got to be a nightmare for you, and I won't be arrogant enough to stand here and tell you I understand how you feel. But you must believe me . . . I can do this job best alone." Putting his strong hands on Millie Jordan's shoulders, he added, "Ma'am, Raven Morrow will kill your boy for sure if she gets any hint that she's being followed—and two riders are twice as easy to spot as one."

The redhead said nothing, although the look in her eyes showed that she disagreed with the lawman's plan.

Giving her shoulders a reassuring squeeze, Tug Farrell left the supervision of collecting the supplies to Deputy Ed Willis. Farrell needed to see the governor and tell him what had happened and then send a wire to the chief U.S. marshal in Denver, informing Clyde that Vic Devlin had been caught and jailed, but the marshal was once again in pursuit of Raven Morrow and Clete Hobbs.

# Chapter Ten

By two-thirty in the afternoon, U.S. Marshal Tug Farrell was ready to travel. Along with the necessary supplies, a new Winchester .44 seven-shot repeater had been donated by Sacramento's gunsmith, and there were several boxes of cartridges in the saddlebags.

A crowd had gathered to wish the marshal good luck. Just before he swung into the saddle, Farrell said to Deputy Ed Willis, "Take good care of Vic Devlin for me, Ed. The man's a wild beast," the marshal warned. "Watch him close, and don't take any chances with him."

"Got it," Willis assured him grimly.

Millie Jordan stepped beside Farrell and declared, "Marshal, I want to thank you for your concern over my son." Fighting to keep her composure, she bit down hard on her lower lip.

Tug Farrell reached for her shoulders. "Mrs. Jordan," he said softly, "I *will* bring Tommy back to you. Try to keep your chin up. Okay?"

"I'll try," Millie responded, blinking against her tears. "I . . . I just wish I could go with you."

"Like I said, ma'am, it would be too dangerous." With that, the ruggedly handsome U.S. marshal swung into the saddle and rode north out of Sacramento.

Deputy Ed Willis returned to the sheriff's office, grieved by the loss of his fellow lawmen—and feeling the full weight of the job, now that he was responsible until a new sheriff could be elected. After spending a

few minutes in the office, he strolled back to the jail to
check on his prisoners.

When Willis stepped into the cell area, Vic Devlin
rose from his bunk and moved to the bars. "What's goin'
on out there?" he asked. "I heard all the shootin' earlier.
Sounded like a war had broken out."

Seeing no reason the outlaw should not know, the
deputy gave him the details, then explained that Tug
Farrell had ridden north out of town in pursuit of the
gang.

"I see," Devlin mused. "Well, those scum he's after
left me here, refused to take me with them"—he
grinned—"so, believe it or not, I hope he catches 'em."

Just before sunset, U.S. Marshal Tug Farrell picked
up the outlaws' trail. Well-seasoned at reading sign, he
could tell that Raven Morrow was pushing hard, apparently heading for Oregon. When darkness began to fall
and he was no longer able to track the gang, he made
camp for the night.

At the same time Tug Farrell was making camp,
Raven Morrow and her gang hauled up in a grove of
trees. Sitting quietly, they studied a farmhouse, its window filled with the warm glow of lamplight, a hundred
yards away across a meadow.

"Okay," Raven began, looking at her men and
Maude Esther Dodd in the gathering gloom, "we're
going inside that nice, isolated place. We'll kill whoever's in there, then take the place over for the night."
She smiled gleefully, adding, "Hopefully they'll have
some decent food. I'm starving."

Tommy Jordan, who sat on Raven's saddle in front
of her, began to whimper.

"Shut up, kid!" snapped Raven, sinking her fingers
into the boy's thick red hair and shaking his head.
"That's enough out of you, you hear me?"

Maude Esther inched her horse close and said
calmly, "Raven, the boy's goin' through a pretty tough
experience. Aren't you bein' a little hard on him?"

Raven glared at the portly woman. Her voice was

as cold as ice as she retorted, "Don't tell me what to do, Maude Esther." Then, giving her gang a sweeping glance, she ordered, "Come on. Let's go."

They rode into the yard of the small farmhouse, dismounting in a hurry. She shoved the boy at Maude Esther, ordering in a harsh whisper, "Here. Take care of him." Pointing at Mack Dugan and Earl Penrod, she told them, "You two stay here. And you men"—she indicated Linus Meade, Floyd Thorpe, and Bert Wade —"go around to the back door and make sure no one comes out." Then she strode onto the front porch with Clete Hobbs and Jack Bullard and kicked open the door, racing through the house with weapons drawn to where the family was preparing supper in the kitchen.

The family—mother, father, and two teenage boys —stood transfixed by the sight of the armed intruders. Then the farmer found his voice and fixed Raven with a hot look, demanding, "What do you mean, barging into my house like this? What do you want?"

"Supper," she replied coldly, and shot him through the heart.

His wife screamed and dashed to her husband as he collapsed on the floor. Their older son reacted quickly, as if his fury crowded out all fear. Darting toward the corner near the back door, he grabbed for a rifle leaning there. But Jack Bullard immediately swung his gun on the youth and fired. The boy took the slug in his lower right side and stumbled against a straight-backed chair, knocking it over. Breathing hard through clenched teeth, he clutched his wounded side and staggered with determination toward the rifle. Grinning maliciously, Bullard declared, "Tough little bugger, ain't you?" and fired again, killing the youth.

The younger boy stood frozen with horror, too stunned to even scream. His mother, as if propelled by a will other than her own, stood up and stepped to the counter, grabbing a twelve-inch butcher knife. Eyes wild, she raised the weapon and walked like a zombie toward Raven Morrow.

"Watch her, Raven!" gasped Clete Hobbs, who stood in the doorway.

"Don't worry, Clete," the brunette replied. Sneering wickedly, she cocked her revolver, aiming it at the woman's heart, and waited for her to come closer. Raven's demonic dark eyes watched her adversary intently, and when the woman was but three feet away, she fired. Blood spurted from the woman's heart and she fell in a heap.

Raven then turned toward the last remaining family member. The boy inched away from her, his face white with terror. A deathly stillness settled over the big smoke-filled kitchen. Finally the boy choked out, "Please! Please don't kill me! Please!"

There was a cold amusement on Raven Morrow's face as she raised her gun. The teenager stiffened, waiting for the inevitable, his lips moving in silent prayer until, squeezing the trigger, the woman shot him in the forehead. His head snapped back from the impact, propelling him against the counter. Then, his body as slack as a rag doll, he slid off the counter and sprawled on the floor.

Breaking open her revolver, Raven punched out the spent shells. While doing so, she called, "Okay, the rest of you can come in now!"

Thorpe, Wade, and Meade filed into the kitchen through the back door, their darting eyes taking in the carnage. Dugan and Penrod came in from the front, leaving Maude Esther Dodd out on the porch with Tommy Jordan, who was quivering with fright.

To Thorpe, Wade, and Meade, Raven said, "You boys pick up these bodies and dump them out front. I don't want to have to look at corpses while I'm eating— nor do I want to see them out the window tomorrow morning over breakfast." The three new gang members quickly obeyed. Looking around, Raven noted that the older woman and the boy were not inside, and she called, "Maude Esther! Come on in here and get to work. The farmer's wife had supper already started—

looks like beef stew. Add some more to it so there's enough for all of us. And snap to it! I'm hungry."

Tommy Jordan had his head buried in Maude Esther's skirt while the bodies were carried out and tossed off the front porch. When the men had gone back inside, the middle-aged woman squeezed the boy's shoulder reassuringly. "Come on, son. Best to do what she says. Just try to ignore the blood—and for heaven's sake, try not to cry. It makes Raven angry when you cry. Okay?"

Tommy's teeth were chattering so hard he could not speak. But he nodded, walking closely beside Maude Esther as they entered the house.

Sitting the boy on a chair at the table, Maude Esther then went to the stove to finish cooking the meal that had been started. Raven plopped down in a chair across from Tommy Jordan, who sat with his head bowed and his eyes fixed on his lap. The outlaw leader lit a cigarillo and began chatting happily with her men. Soon all of them were gaily smoking and talking, waiting for their meal.

Maude Esther suddenly began rummaging through the cupboard, searching for something. "What are you looking for?" queried the hard-eyed brunette.

"I need some more flour for the gravy," replied the older woman, continuing her search.

Raven twisted in her chair. Gesturing at a ladder leading up to an opening at one end of the kitchen ceiling, she remarked, "That's probably where they keep their stores. No doubt there'd be a sack of flour up there." Looking across the table at Tommy, she commanded, "Hey, kid. Climb up there and see if you can find a sack of flour."

Tommy raised his head. Immediately obeying, he scooted off his chair, hurried to the ladder, and climbed up. One of the gang members handed him a kerosene lamp, and the boy placed it on the floor of the loft, then pulled himself in. Suddenly he froze in place on his hands and knees. Curled up in a corner under the pitched roof, terrified, was a teenage girl.

Tommy swallowed hard, sent a quick glance in the direction from which he had come, then looked back at her. Quickly he mouthed silently, "Flour?"

She pointed to a stack of cloth flour sacks near a large can of lard. Nodding, he crawled over to the pile and grabbed hold of the top sack, then began to drag it back to the opening.

Raven's voice cut the air. "Hey, kid! What are you doing up there?"

Tommy quickly stuck his face through the opening and said, "Getting a sack of flour, just as you asked."

Jack Bullard stood below while Tommy dropped the sack to him; then the boy climbed down the ladder and returned to his seat at the table. He stared at his lap even more fixedly than before.

While eating the dead family's food, the gang discussed their plans. Raven told them they would gather more men along the way to British Columbia. She intended to move into a mine that was already being worked, kill its occupants, and take it over. Once things were running smoothly, they would kidnap men for slave labor as they had done in the past. If the mines were producing as well as she had heard, they would all get filthy rich.

Swallowing a mouthful of stew, Clete Hobbs told the group, "We need to start watching our back trail."

Jack Bullard guffawed. "What for? Ain't no way they're gonna send a posse after what Raven told 'em she'd do to the kid!"

"I'm not thinking posse, Jack," replied Hobbs stiffly. "I'm thinking Tug Farrell. I know the dude well. He'll be coming after us—you can count on it."

A sour look clouded Raven Morrow's beautiful face. "I wish I'd had the chance to kill that stinking tin star before we left Sacramento." The brunette took another bite of food, then commented, "But you're right, Clete. Farrell will show up for sure." Then, laughing, she sank her fingers into Tommy's hair, shook his head roughly, and declared, "But we've got an edge on Farrell. We've got the brat!"

Tommy suddenly began to cry, saying, "Please take me back to my mother! Please! I want to go home!"

Raven's face stiffened. Throwing down the fork she held in her other hand, she blared, "Shut up, brat! I'm sick and tired of your squalling like a baby!" She shook his head even more roughly.

The more forcefully Raven shook Tommy's head, the louder his cries became. Abruptly she slapped him across the face with an open-handed blow. Tommy peeled off the chair and landed on the floor. No one moved as the furious brunette leaned down and lifted the boy by the front of his shirt. Slapping him forcefully several more times, she then slammed him down on his chair.

Tommy was breathing loudly, biting his lip so hard in a desperate attempt not to cry that it began to bleed. The skin of his face was dead white beneath the red handprints, and his eyes were wild with terror.

"Now, sit up there and eat your supper!" Raven bellowed. "I want you alive and well when Farrell shows up. You're my edge, and I intend to keep it!"

Maude Esther reached under the table, out of Raven's sight, and patted the boy's knee reassuringly. She gave the child a surreptitious look of concern, then went back to eating, and said nothing.

The room was unnaturally silent for a long moment. Then Jack Bullard spoke up, asking Raven if she knew how to travel to reach the southern tip of the Selkirk Mountains where the mines were situated. Turning her attention to her henchman, she explained that the Selkirk range was actually a part of the Rocky Mountains just west of the Continental Divide, which was the natural border between the provinces of British Columbia and Alberta. The gold mines, she told Bullard, were located in British Columbia between the mountain towns of Trail and Cranbrook, near Kokanee Glacier.

Mack Dugan asked, "How come we ain't goin' back to the mine in the Sierras?"

Shaking her head with a look of long-suffering

piety, Raven said, "Don't you remember anything, Mack? I told you before we were captured that the mine in the Sierras would soon play out anyway—not to mention it's much too close for comfort to civilization . . . and lawmen."

"Oh, right," Dugan responded, contrite. "How long do you figure it'll take us to get there?"

The brunette shoved her chair back from the table, stuck a cigarillo in her mouth, and replied, "Well, from Sacramento to the mines is just about nine hundred miles. It's now late October, so we could run into some light snow in Oregon and maybe heavier stuff in Washington." Pausing, she snapped her fingers at Clete Hobbs and ordered, "Give me a match."

Hobbs fished one from a shirt pocket and lit the tip of the cigarillo for her.

Raven drew in a lungful of smoke, blew it out in a long stream, then proceeded. "We'll probably hit the real deep snow after we pass a small settlement known as Spokane Falls, which is about a hundred and forty miles south of the mines. Taking everything into consideration, I'd say we'll reach the mines around the middle of December."

Bullard belched and leaned back in his chair. "We'll have to pull a few robberies along the way to keep us in food and supplies."

"That's right," Raven agreed.

"Nine hundred miles," sighed Earl Penrod. "That's a long stretch."

"So what?" spoke up Linus Meade. "Most of us been runnin' from the hangman's noose for a long time. We've covered a lot more than nine hundred miles just tryin' to elude the long arm of the law." He smiled, showing a mouthful of rotted teeth. "And it'll be worth the trip, once we get our hands on all that gold!"

Raven stood and smiled. "That's right." She stretched and yawned. "Well, boys, I'm looking forward to spending the night in a real bed—not to mention getting out of this prison garb. That older kid, he looked to be about my size, so I'm going to outfit myself in his

clothes." She grinned and looked down at her feet. "It
was right friendly of Sheriff Sovern to let me keep my
riding boots, don't you think?" With the laughter of her
men echoing through the house, Raven Morrow left the
kitchen and headed off to sleep.

U.S. Marshal Tug Farrell had ridden about ten
miles from where he camped the night before when the
trail led him to the isolated farmhouse. Sitting under
the protective cover of the same stand of trees that had
sheltered Raven Morrow and her gang from view, the
lawman assessed the house across the meadow. All
seemed quiet.

Riding closer, he could see someone sitting on the
porch. Getting nearer still, he saw it was a young girl,
small in stature but probably twelve or thirteen, with
her blond hair in pigtails. At the sound of his horse's
hoofbeats, her head snapped up and she got to her feet
with a look of terror on her face. It was then that Farrell
saw the four blanket-covered forms just beyond the
porch. Farrell's stomach turned over. He was certain
that Raven Morrow and her gang had been there—and
that under the blankets lay lifeless evidence of that.

The girl started backing toward the doorway, when
he held his jacket aside and revealed his badge. Relaxing, she moved back to the edge of the porch, clasp-
ing her hands in front of her. The big, broad-shoulderd
man eased from his saddle and gazed at the covered
bodies. Touching his hat brim, he said to the girl, whose
eyes were swollen from weeping, "Good morning, little
lady. I'm United States Marshal Tug Farrell. What's
your name?"

"Marsha Burley, sir," she replied in a tiny voice.
Tears spilled over her lids as she added, "My parents
and my two brothers were murdered last night." She
paused. "I covered them up so I didn't have to look at
them."

He looked at the forlorn young girl with compas-
sion, sick at heart for her. Crouching down so he could

look her in the eye, he asked gently, "The people who
did this, were they a bunch of men and two women?"

"Yes, sir. I think there were seven men—at least, I
heard one of the women, the woman with the long
black hair, mention seven different names. She was the
meanest of all. Her name is Raven. She talked about
you. I heard her say she wants to kill you."

"I don't doubt it, Marsha," Farrell responded
grimly. "Did they have a boy with them?"

"Yes, sir. The mean woman beat him."

Taking her small hands in his, the lawman asked,
"Why didn't they kill you, honey?"

"They didn't know I was here," Marsha responded
shakily. "When they came into our house just before
supper last night, I was in the loft above the kitchen.
Mama"—she sniffed back tears—"Mama had sent me
up there to bring some supplies down."

"So you stayed hidden in the loft and they didn't
know you were there?"

"Yes, sir. They sent the boy up there to find some
flour and he saw me, but he never let on."

"Did you see any of the shooting, Marsha?"

The girl's chin quivered. "Only when the woman
called Raven shot my father. I didn't look down again
until after they left this morning. Then I came down
and . . . and . . ."

Marsha Burley broke down and sobbed. Tug Farrell
took her into his arms and tried to comfort her as best
he could. Finally her weeping subsided, and he handed
her his handkerchief.

Drying her face and blowing her nose, the young
blonde said, "I don't know what to do, Marshal. I just
don't know what to do."

"Is there anyone you can go and live with?"

"I have relatives back East, but no one around
here."

"Are there some neighbors you could stay with until your relatives are notified?"

She thought for a moment. "Yes, sir. I'm sure the

Peabodys would take me in. They have a farm about four miles east of here."

"I'll take you there." Glancing at the bodies, he asked, "Would you like for me to bury your parents and brothers first?"

"That won't be necessary, thank you," replied the girl. "I'm sure Mr. Peabody will ask some of the other neighboring farmers to help him take care of it." Pausing, she asked, "How long have you been after that gang, Marshal?"

"That's a long story, honey," Farrell sighed. "Tell me, did you hear them call one of the men Clete?"

"Yes, sir."

"Well, I've been after Raven and Clete for over three years. The others have joined with them since. The boy's name is Tommy Jordan. They kidnapped him in Sacramento."

Marsha nodded. "I heard them say that. And they know you're coming after them. They said so. Raven put it that she had an edge on you since she had Tommy . . . only she called him the brat."

Farrell sniffed and said sardonically, "Yeah, she's not exactly the motherly type." He stood up. "Tell you what. Why don't you go get your horse, and I'll . . . I'll put your family inside the house. We wouldn't want any animals finding them before your neighbors can return."

The girl looked over at the blanket-covered forms and stared at them for a long moment, tears trickling down her cheeks. Then she hurried toward the barn, her head lowered.

After placing the four bodies inside the house and saddling the girl's horse, the twosome rode eastward toward the Peabody place. Turning to Marsha, Farrell asked, "What time did the gang ride out?"

"At dawn, sir. They were in a real hurry to get going. I stayed in the loft until I was sure they were gone for good."

"I assume you heard them talking."

"Yes, sir. Most of the time. Sometimes I was so

scared and upset, I almost screamed. My mind wasn't too clear then."

"Did you hear them say where they were going?"

"To Canada."

"Canada?" echoed the marshal in surprise.

"British Columbia. That Raven woman said something about gold mines. She said they're going to kidnap men and make them work in their mine like slaves."

"Did they say where in British Columbia?"

Marsha's face screwed up in thought. "I . . . I can't remember for sure. Are there some Dunkirk Mountains in British Columbia?"

"Not that I know of," replied Farrell. He thought for a moment, then remarked, "But there are some *Selkirk* Mountains just over the border."

"That's it!" exclaimed the pigtailed girl. "Selkirk!"

By the time Marsha Burley had been deposited with the Peabodys, who assured Tug Farrell that they would take care of her until relatives in the East could be notified, it was midafternoon before the U.S. marshal was back on the outlaws' trail. Riding hard, he reached the town of Marysville a half hour before sundown. Upon entering a café, he learned that the Morrow gang had robbed Marysville's general store of food and camping supplies. They had also stolen a packhorse at gunpoint from the hostler. Asking what time the gang had ridden out of Marysville, Farrell learned that they were better than five hours ahead of him.

Wanting to gain time on the gang, Farrell galloped out of Marysville, pushing his sorrel hard. After a long stretch, he slowed the animal to a fast walk, taking a few moments to admire his surroundings. Looking to his left, he enjoyed the brilliant red and orange of the sunset, and while running his gaze the full length of its beauty, he caught movement on the periphery of his vision. He twisted in the saddle to focus on the dark object about a half-mile behind him, and saw that it was a lone rider. The rider was briefly illuminated by a ray of sunlight, and Farrell's keen eyes determined the man was riding a bay. Seconds later the rider dipped into a draw, out of sight.

Farrell faced forward once again, forgetting him. He put the sorrel to a steady canter until it was too dark to read sign, and then, pulling into a small clearing surrounded by heavy brush, he made camp.

# Chapter Eleven

Skirting the foothills of the towering Sierra Nevadas, whose highest peaks were glistening with fresh snow, Raven Morrow and her gang continued pushing north. Bringing up the rear, Earl Penrod kept an eye on their back trail. Raven continued to carry Tommy Jordan on her horse so she could threaten his life if Tug Farrell showed up. The boy's head, neck, and face were spotted with bruises from the beatings she had given him for crying. Maude Esther Dodd's face showed her disapproval of the way the brunette was treating the boy, but so far she had held her peace.

When darkness began to fall, the gang hauled up in a wooded draw and set up camp. Maude Esther unpacked the cooking utensils and the men broke out the bedrolls. Tommy Jordan was helping Maude Esther when Raven approached him and snapped, "Hey, kid. Get busy and gather branches for the fire. You'll find plenty lying around."

Fear showed in Tommy's eyes as he nodded and turned to obey. Maude Esther laid down a pan and a skillet that she had in her hands and said, "I'll help you, Tommy."

Raven gave the big woman a sharp look and said harshly, "Let him do it himself!"

The Dodd woman retorted, "Raven, it's getting dark. The woods are pretty spooky this time of day. He's been frightened enough. I'll just—"

"Don't argue with me, woman! Your job is to cook!"

Maude Esther bristled, but she said nothing more. Her face stiff with anger, she returned to her task.

Walking past where the men were gathered, Tommy Jordan began picking up broken limbs and branches. He carried two armloads over to where Maude Esther needed her cooking fire, and then he walked into the woods again. He was deep in the trees when he looked back through the gloom to the campsite—and he suddenly realized that no one could even see him amid the trees.

Frightened of the mean and brutal woman, he decided this was his chance to escape. He would rather face what dangers might await him alone in the wilderness than to be beaten all the time. Taking a deep breath, he whirled and headed farther into the woods, weaving among the trees and brush by what little light remained and running hard to the south.

A quarter-hour had passed before Raven drew near the fire and asked Maude Esther, "Where's the brat?"

The big woman was on her knees, stirring beans in a pan. Glancing at Raven over her shoulder, she replied, "I don't know. Must be havin' a hard time findin' more wood."

"I don't think so," mused Raven, running her gaze over the area. "I think my little friend has flown the coop."

While she spoke, the brunette moved to the men and told them Tommy had run away. Ordering Jack Bullard and Clete Hobbs to carry the two lanterns they had with them, she instructed the men to split into two groups and make a wide circle. She and Maude Esther would remain at the campsite.

As the seven men were about to take up the search, Raven growled, "Don't come back without the kid."

The men eyed each other by the light of the fire. Raven needed Tommy Jordan as a tool to ward off Tug Farrell—and she would be one uncontrollable hellcat if they returned empty-handed.

When both teams of men had disappeared into the

heavy timber, Maude Esther turned to the brunette and, her voice lighthearted, asked, "Go easy on the kid, won't you? After all, you were a child once, Raven. Don't you remember getting frightened?"

Raven's fury was uncontained. "How dare you tell me what to do!" she raged, spittle flying from her mouth. "That brat is going to get a beating within an inch of his life—and if you like *your* face the way it is, you'd better keep out of it! You got that?"

Although Maude Esther was almost twice Raven's size, the smaller woman's erratic behavior was so intimidating that practically everyone—with the exception of Tug Farrell—feared her. Whether it was her utter lack of conscience or her deadly temper, Raven Morrow was not someone to cross.

Young Tommy Jordan stopped to catch his breath, leaning against a tree. Looking up through the treetops, he could see the early stars winking in the heavens. It was getting so dark, he could hardly see a foot in front of his face. Pushing away from the tree, he stumbled a few more steps, then tripped over something on the ground. He quickly regained his feet and, blinking against the gloom, decided to find a spot under some brush where he could curl up for the night, then start out again when dawn began breaking.

He took a few more steps, when he heard voices behind him. His spine tingled. They were coming after him! Looking back, he could make out tiny flashes of light, and he knew instantly that it was a lantern that someone was carrying. Panicking, he whirled and ran for all he was worth, but a tree brushed his shoulder, throwing him off balance. His feet tangled, and he went down in a rolling heap.

Tommy's lungs felt as though they were on fire as he scrambled to his feet and ran again. In the darkness he plunged into a thicket, and the limbs seemed to grasp him and claw at him angrily. He cried out in fear, then fell, and he lay prostrate, gasping for breath and trying to squelch the panic that was clogging his throat.

Above the wheeze of his burning lungs he could hear the voices getting louder, and he got to his knees and saw the bobbing light of the lantern drawing closer.

The terrified boy began to whimper, speaking to his mother and asking for her help. On his feet again, he darted into the black void ahead of him, using every ounce of strength he could throw into his legs. He had gone some fifty or sixty feet when suddenly he collided with the trunk of a tree.

Stunned, Tommy Jordan fell backward to the ground. His nose hurt and his head was spinning. Rolling over, he rose to his hands and knees, shaking his head. Then he heard Jack Bullard's booming voice shouting, "Tommy! Tommy! No sense tryin' to hide, kid! We'll find you! Come on out! Save us all a lot of trouble!"

He could hear the rustling of feet on leaves and twigs. It sounded very close. Still on his hands and knees, he raised his eyes and saw the lantern in the big man's hand as the group pressed through the trees straight toward him. Suddenly one of the men shouted, "There he is!"

Though his exhausted young body had been pushed to the limit, Tommy Jordan refused to give up. As the dark forms loomed over him, he spun around and spent what was left of his energy in a useless crawl.

Abruptly, powerful hands grabbed him and lifted him off the ground. "Gotcha, kid!" exclaimed Floyd Thorpe, overwhelming the boy as if he had the arms of an octopus. "That sure was a stupid move. Now you gotta go back and face Raven."

Reaching the campsite, Thorpe handed the boy over triumphantly. "Here he is, Raven," the man said proudly.

Raven Morrow glared down at the child, whose entire body quaked with fear. Tommy flicked a glance toward Maude Esther Dodd for help, but she made no move. "Forget it, brat," Raven snarled, noticing the beseeching look in his eyes. "No one's gonna help you." She stood over Tommy, her body rigid. "So you thought you could get away, huh?" she snarled. "Well, I'm going to teach you that you can't get away with anything so long as I've got you!" Snapping her fingers at Jack Bullard, she ordered, "Get me a stick. A big one."

Like a trained dog, Bullard darted about, searching for the desired object.

Tommy trembled uncontrollably, whimpering in terror.

"So you want to cry some more, huh?" hissed Raven. "Well, I'm going to give you something to cry about! Nobody runs away from me, brat! Nobody!"

Bullard stepped over to Raven and handed her a three-foot limb. Gripping it hard in her right hand, Raven raised it over her head.

"No!" screamed Tommy, raising his arms to fend off the coming blow.

Ignoring him, the brunette brought the stick down savagely across the boy's shoulder, and his knees buckled just before the blow struck, lessening its impact. He dropped to the ground, protecting his head with his arms as Raven lashed him repeatedly wherever she could make the stick connect.

Without warning, Maude Esther Dodd dashed over to Raven, seizing the stick and yanking it from her grip. In one smooth move the big woman raised a knee and broke the stick over it. "That's enough!" she shrieked, tossing the two pieces into the fire. "You keep that up and you'll kill him! Then where will you be? I thought you wanted to keep him alive as insurance!"

There was a collective intake of breath from the other gang members as everyone waited for Raven's reaction. But the big woman's audacious act had apparently left Raven momentarily stunned, and she stared at Maude Esther incredulously. There was no sound other than the crackling fire. Maude Esther then turned from Raven and knelt beside the weeping boy, whose body was knotted up on the ground, speaking consoling words to him.

It was as if the portly woman's movement broke a spell that had fallen over Raven. Her demonic eyes bore into the older woman as she threatened in a voice all

the more terrifying for its matter-of-factness, "Maude
Esther, if you ever interfere with anything I do again,
you are going to be very sorry."

Midmorning the next day Raven Morrow and her
gang rode into a small northern California town called
Paradise. The men wanted to stop for a drink and, haul-
ing up in front of the Rusty Lantern Saloon, they dismounted and went inside. After warning Tommy to
keep his mouth shut while they were in the saloon, the
brunette got off her horse and yanked Tommy to the
ground. She was about to propel him into the saloon
when Maude Esther suggested, "Raven, why don't I just
keep Tommy out here? You go on in and have your
drink."

Raven thought about the suggestion a moment,
then shrugged. "Okay, but don't you go anywhere. We
won't be in there very long." When Maude Esther assured her they would sit down on the boardwalk and
wait, Raven adjusted the gun belt on her waist and
pushed her way into the saloon.

Her men were sitting around two adjacent tables,
and the bartender was carrying them a couple of bottles
of whiskey and several glasses on a tray. There were
patrons at several other tables, and the bar was lined
with men standing shoulder to shoulder. As the beautiful brunette made her way to the tables where her men
were seated, every man turned to eye her, staring hard
for a few moments; then they went back to their drinks.

Sitting down between Clete Hobbs and Jack Bullard, she picked up the bottle of whiskey that was making the rounds and held it toward the light. "Looks like
cheap stuff to me."

Clete Hobbs took the bottle from her and scruti-
nized it carefully, then announced, "I don't see anything wrong with it."

Mack Dugan suggested, "I'll get you some better
stuff, Raven." He jumped up, eager to please his boss,
then made his way to the bar. The small, wiry Dugan
stood behind two much larger men and tapped one of

them on the shoulder, saying, "I need to order somethin' from the bartender."

The men looked over their shoulders and eyed him
scornfully, and one of them said, "You'll have to wait
your turn, pal."

"Look, I just want to order something and take it to
the table."

The smaller of the duo looked Dugan up and down
and asked, "You wantin' trouble, are you, buddy?"

Dugan looked him square in the eye and retorted,
"I wasn't, but it looks like maybe I've found it anyhow."

The man's bigger friend turned around and faced
Dugan. Cuffing him hard on the shoulder, he snarled,
"You've found it, all right! I'm gonna pound you into the
floor!"

Raven and her cohorts saw what was happening,
and when Jack Bullard saw the big man shove Dugan,
he started out of his chair. But Raven stood up and
waved him off, then hurried to the bar.

Seeing the captivating woman coming his way,
Dugan's challenger grinned and said to him, "I'll take
care of you in a minute. First things first." He appraised
Raven lustfully, then said, "Well, well, beautiful. What
can we do for you?"

Raven smiled pleasantly, and in a sweet voice asked
the larger of the two men, "What seems to be the problem here, fellas?"

"No problem *now*, you fine beauty."

Her smile vanished and she snarled, "Good, because my man came to the bar to get me some decent
whiskey, and you're preventing it! Now, move your
ugly carcasses!"

Obviously startled by her change in attitude, the
man bobbed his head. Then, recovering, he laughed
and declared, "You don't fool me with that tough act,
lady. I think what you really want is some lovin'. Let's
start with a kiss."

The men at the bar began to whistle and make
catcalls as the man reached for Raven Morrow. But she

adeptly stepped back and hissed, "Don't you dare touch me!"

Ignoring her tone, the man's friend lumbered toward her, insisting, "We'll both get us a kiss!"

Suddenly Raven's revolver was in her hand. The gun roared twice, sending bullets through one man's right foot and the other's left foot. Both men howled in agony and fell to the floor. By that time, the rest of Raven's men were crowding in, relieving the two men of their guns, then staring down the rest of the patrons, warning them with their expressions not to try anything.

While the two rowdies rolled on the floor, their boots filling with blood, Raven swung her smoking muzzle around the room. "Anybody else here want to play games?"

Nobody moved, and nobody replied.

Raven turned back to the bar and caught the bartender's eye. "You got a decent bottle of whiskey, mister?" she asked, clipping her words. "Or is that rotgut you gave my men all you sell?"

"I have some more expensive whiskey, lady," he answered.

"Toss me a bottle."

The bartender took a bottle from under the counter and set it on the bar. "That'll be four dollars," he grunted.

Motioning to Dugan, Raven ordered, "Grab the bottle, Mack. Those two on the floor'll pay for it."

"Hey!" shouted the bartender. "You can't do that! If you take the bottle, you pay for it!"

Raven's gun roared again. The slug whizzed past the bartender's ear, smashing into a large mirror on the wall behind the bar. Glass shattered and crashed to the floor. The bartender's eyes bulged as the woman warned, "I can cut off both your ears from here, mister. Now, do you collect from those two on the floor, or do I operate on your ears?"

"Take the bottle and go!" gasped the bartender.

She smiled wickedly. "That's better." Turning to

her men, she ordered, "Finish your drinks, boys. I think
we've seen enough of Paradise."

At the close of another day, U.S. Marshal Tug Farrell was topping a hill and happened to look behind
him, catching sight of a lone rider coming his way about
two miles back. He thought of the rider he had seen at
sunset the day before, but the distance was too great to
tell if it was the same bay horse.

Finding a grassy spot beside a stream, Farrell made
camp. He built a fire and cooked his supper; then, leaning against a tree and shoveling beans into his mouth,
he smiled to himself. When passing through Paradise
just after noon, he had learned that Raven and her
bunch were now just three hours ahead of him. Unfortunately, though, they were not traveling a straight
course, which meant he had to continuously read sign,
making his pursuit slow and stopping him completely
when darkness fell. He was pleased with his progress,
however. Little by little he was catching up with them.

While washing his cooking utensils in the stream,
the marshal heard his horse nicker. Instinctively he
whipped out his gun and spun around. All was quiet.
Farrell waited a few seconds, holstered the gun, and
finished his task.

While he was laying out his bedroll, Vic Devlin
came to mind. Farrell thought that if Devlin had somehow escaped from the jail in Sacramento, he might just
be trailing him with the intention of putting a bullet in
his back. Was that lone rider Devlin? He tried to shake
off the thought, but because it was a possibility, his
nerves tightened.

Lying in the bedroll under the canopy of twinkling
stars, the lawman let his mind wander to his childhood.
When a mental picture of his father presented itself, the
grief he felt over Maynard Farrell's death rose to the
surface. Suddenly Farrell found himself hoping it *was*
Vic Devlin trailing him. It would give him an excuse to
blow his father's killer to kingdom come.

Farrell's thoughts ran to Raven Morrow and the

wicked bunch he was pursuing. He hoped Tommy Jordan was all right. Thinking about the boy brought lovely Millie Jordan to mind, and he remembered how the sunlight danced in her copper-colored hair.

*I'd like to see her again,* he told himself. *Not just when I return Tommy to her, but maybe over a nice dinner before I head back to Denver. I haven't laid eyes on a woman who has so captivated me since . . . since I was foolish enough to fall in love with Raven Morrow.* Shaking his head, he asked himself how he could have been so taken in by her.

Soon the soft sounds of the night eased his mind and lulled him to sleep. His last conscious thought was of Millie Jordan, and he fell asleep with a smile on his lips.

# Chapter Twelve

Two more days passed, and U.S. Marshal Tug Farrell learned from some travelers who had seen the gang that he was only about two hours behind Raven Morrow and her bunch. Riding steadily through the rugged country, Farrell figured the gang would be rounding the southern tip of the majestic Cascade range, heading through the dense forest in the direction of the great volcanic lava beds just south of the Oregon border. Eager to catch up to them, he pushed his sorrel harder.

Shortly before sundown, the small town of Burney came into view. Following the ingrained habit of looking over his shoulder periodically, the big lawman caught sight of a lone rider about a mile behind him—and the man was definitely on a bay horse. He watched the man's progress for a few moments, then said aloud, "If it's you, Devlin, I'll be ready."

The federal marshal entered Burney and rode up its dusty main street until he came to a livery stable. Farrell left the sorrel with the hostler for a good feeding and a rubdown, and to be bedded down in a stall for the night. His mount taken care of, the lawman headed back down the street to Mary Lou's Café, which he had noticed a half-block to the south.

As he drew abreast of a saloon, not breaking his stride, he glanced cursorily at a group of men clustered on the boardwalk in front of it. He was almost at the café two doors past the saloon when a gruff voice called out, "Sheriff Farrell!"

Halting, the lawman turned around, and it was obvious who had shouted his name. A tough-looking character wearing a tied-down gun on his hip was swaggering toward Farrell, a triumphant sneer on his worn face. The marshal had to study the haggard face a moment before he recognized the man as Curly Stout, whom he had arrested some four years previously for severely beating an elderly woman in a fit of anger. Stout had been given a three-year sentence for assault.

Four men of Stout's caliber followed him as he headed toward Farrell. The marshal's nerves went tight as Stout suddenly stopped, planting his feet. Farrell waited silently for what was to come, and Stout's four friends quickly moved out of the line of fire.

Stout finally broke the silence, saying caustically, "Fancy meetin' you all the way out here in California, Sheriff."

"Marshal," corrected Farrell. "United States marshal. What do you want, Stout?"

The man's words were flat and bitter. "I want your hide."

Passersby began to stop, watching with interest as Farrell warned his challenger, "If you want to live to sleep in your bed, not in the ground, you'd better do a quick about-face and go back to what you were doing before I happened along."

Curly Stout shook his head slowly. "After all the time I've been storin' up hatred for you, I ain't goin' nowhere till I drop you in the dust. I spent three years behind bars 'cause of you, and now that fate has planted your dirty frame in front of me, I'm gonna take advantage of it. Go for your iron!"

"You didn't spend three years in prison because of me," countered Farrell icily. "You're the one who beat up that old woman, not me. I only did my duty and arrested you. Don't blame me for cutting three years out of your life." The marshal paused, then said, "If you force me to draw, Stout, they'll carry you away. Don't push it. Just do like I said and leave."

A flicker in Stout's eyes told Tug Farrell the man's

hand was going to dip for his gun. Within less than a heartbeat, it did.

Farrell fired before Stout could clear leather. The slug tore into the man's chest, exploding his heart, and Curly Stout's dead body slammed to the ground.

Ready for what could come next, the seasoned lawman held his smoking gun steady and looked quickly at each of Stout's four cohorts. Through his teeth he called, "Any of you lizard bellies want to follow your pal through the gates of hell?"

The foursome silently regarded Farrell with hate-filled eyes but then turned and walked away. Relieved, the marshal holstered his gun and continued toward the café. He was about to enter when he spotted the rider on the bay horse trotting toward him. The sun was behind the rider, throwing his face into deep shadow under the broad-brimmed hat he wore. Every nerve in Farrell's body stretched tight. If the man on the bay was Vic Devlin, he wanted to get their showdown over with.

Eager to identify the rider, Farrell stepped off the boardwalk and headed up the middle of the street to meet him. The bay kept coming straight at him. The lawman tensed, his hand ready to go for his gun, when suddenly he blinked and put his hands on his hips, feeling a mixture of relief, anger, and—he had to admit—pleasure. Visible now underneath the hat was the lovely face of Millie Jordan, her long copper tresses flowing behind her shoulders.

Millie reined in and stared down at the rugged lawman with a look of stubborn determination. Before he could speak, she said, "Don't tell me to turn around and go back, Marshal Farrell. I've been following you for days, and now that I've worked up the nerve to show myself, I am not about to go home. I'm riding with you until Tommy is rescued."

Tug Farrell was not about to let the beautiful red-head know that he was secretly glad to see her. His voice scolding, he told her, "Mrs. Jordan, since you've chosen to ignore everything I've told you about how dangerous this mission is, I insist that you take a room at that hotel over there and stay put until I return with Tommy."

Millie's back stiffened. Jutting her delicate jaw, she replied sharply, "That shiny badge you wear may entitle you to a lot of things, Marshal, but ordering me around is not one of them. I am *not* going to hole up in that hotel and just twiddle my thumbs."

The bay was bobbing its head. Reaching out and taking hold of the bridle to steady the animal, Farrell shrugged and said, "Well, ma'am, you're right. I can't order you to stay at the hotel—but I *can* keep you from traveling with me."

"Fine," she retorted. "Then I'll just keep following you as I have been, a mile or two behind . . . even though it's terribly dangerous for a woman to travel alone in the wilderness."

The rugged lawman had to force himself to keep from laughing, knowing full well that she was manipulating him. He threw up his hands and sighed. "Okay, okay. I can see it's useless to argue with you. Let's bring your horse over to the livery stable and let the hostler tend to him, and we'll eat our own supper at Mary Lou's Café over there, then get rooms for the night at the hotel. It'll be too dark to read sign before much longer, so seeing as how we managed to reach a town at sundown, we may as well be comfortable for a change. We'll head out at the crack of dawn."

The vivacious redhead smiled slowly. "Now you're showing the intelligence I thought you had," she announced, swinging down from the saddle.

They led her mount up the street, leaving it in the hostler's care, then headed back to Mary Lou's Café. As Farrell guided her by the elbow toward the door of the café, Millie glanced at the men carrying away the body of Curly Stout. "I heard a gunshot while coming into town, Marshal, and I believe I saw you holstering your gun right afterward. Are you by any chance responsible for that man's, uh, condition?"

"Yes, ma'am," he admitted, opening the café door.

"To make a long story short, let's just say that fella was carrying a grudge for being sent to jail a few years ago, and he wanted to get even."

Passing through the doorway in front of him, Millie remarked, "I guess he didn't succeed."

"It's all in how you look at it," Farrell responded dryly.

During the meal, the marshal encouraged Millie Jordan by telling her they should catch up to the gang by the end of the next day. Tommy would soon be rescued.

Millie's face suddenly crumpled. "Oh, Marshal," she choked, fighting back tears, "what if they've hurt him, or—"

Farrell instinctively reached across the table and took hold of her hand. Squeezing it tight, he said tenderly, "Tommy's all right, Mrs. Jordan. I know it. Soon you'll have your son back home where he belongs."

She squeezed his hand back, managing a faint smile. "Thank you," she breathed.

Farrell released her hand, and they started eating again.

As soon as they had finished their meal, the lawman and the beautiful redhead got up and left the café. They had just stepped outside when Farrell grabbed Millie's arm and stopped. Four dark figures emerged from the shadows, coming at them from two sides—the men who had been with Curly Stout.

Seeing murder in their eyes, Farrell knew they meant to kill him, and he had to act fast before they got him in a cross fire. His hand went for his gun at the same instant he shoved Millie to the ground. She squealed in surprise at the sudden jolt, but the sound was immediately obscured as the whole street seemed to explode into gunfire.

Farrell took out the man farthest to his right as he dove into the street, away from Millie Jordan, and hit the ground himself. While rolling to evade the bullets that were coming his way, he shot another of his attackers. Guns roared and bullets plowed dirt as the veteran lawman evaded them by rolling back and forth, firing when he was sure his aim would be true. Another of the marshal's bullets found its mark, killing the third man.

The fourth man's gun roared, and Farrell immediately felt as though a white-hot poker had been laid on his left thigh. Gritting his teeth, he took aim and winged his last foe in the right shoulder. The man staggered, dropping his gun. When he recovered and reached for the fallen weapon, gripping his wounded shoulder with his left hand, Tug Farrell lined his muzzle on the man's chest and pulled the trigger. There was only the hollow sound of metal on metal.

Cursing himself for not filling the empty chamber of his Colt .45 after dropping Curly Stout, the marshal quickly crawled to the first man he had killed and jerked the revolver from his limp fingers just as the fourth man palmed his gun and was attempting to raise it. The wounded man fired, but his injury threw off his aim and the slug chewed dirt four feet from its target.

Taking careful aim, Farrell fired, and the bullet drilled into the man's chest, smashing the breath out of him. He staggered backward into the hitch rail, leaning against it. Gasping, he coughed, and blood bubbled from his mouth, streaming down his stubbled chin. But he did not relinquish his gun.

Farrell struggled to his feet. Balancing himself on his good leg, he thumbed back the hammer of his weapon and waited to see what the man was going to do.

The man stared fixedly at the marshal.

Tug Farrell stood swaying on his good leg. His wounded leg throbbed with excruciating pain, and he could feel the blood running into his boot. Suddenly his adversary slowly brought up his gun.

Aiming his own weapon at the man's heart, Farrell yelled, "Don't do it, fella! You don't have to die!"

"But *you* do!" grunted the hardcase.

Farrell fired. The man winced with the impact, jarred the hitch rail as his full weight slammed against it, then staggered forward two steps. The revolver slipped from his fingers, and he doubled over, coughing blood, then dropped like a sack of rags on top of his gun. As soon as the man had fallen, the lawman sagged to one knee.

The townspeople who had gathered out of the line of fire to watch swarmed over the street like a colony of ants. Millie Jordan ran toward the marshal and, putting an arm around Farrell, the redhead yelled to the crowd, "Somebody help me get him to a doctor!"

Four men immediately sprang to his service. They carried him to Dr. Jeremiah Winslow's office, and the physician determined that the slug was buried in the thigh and had to come out immediately.

An hour later, Dr. Winslow opened the door to the small waiting room and said to Millie Jordan, "You can come in now, ma'am."

Millie brushed past the elderly physician to where the U.S. marshal lay on the operating table. His pant leg was slit all the way up, and the thigh was heavily bandaged. Farrell's face was colorless, and although he was in great pain, he tried to smile when he saw her standing over him.

Looking into the big man's eyes, Millie said in a voice filled with astonishment, "You were remarkable, taking out those four men like that!"

"Had to work fast," he replied, holding her gaze. "They meant business."

Winslow moved beside them and told the redhead, "The marshal's lucky, Mrs. Farrell. The slug didn't hit the bone—but nonetheless it chewed up the muscle pretty bad."

Millie blushed. "Oh, I'm not the marshal's wife, Doctor."

Winslow's bushy white eyebrows arched. "Oh? The way I got it, the two of you are traveling together."

Millie quickly explained the situation. The doctor then nodded and remarked, "Well, there won't be any traveling for the marshal for at least three weeks."

Farrell was weak, but the words came out strong. "Three weeks! Doc, I can't lie around this town three weeks! Mrs. Jordan's son is in grave danger. I've got outlaws to run down. There's no way—"

"I'm not the one who put the slug in your leg, son," cut in Winslow, "I'm just the guy who took it out. So don't get mad at me. And I say you'll tear the whole thing open if you don't give that wound a chance to heal. It's going to need the attention of a physician every day for the first week. Are you going to tell me you'll be able to find a doctor every day where you'll be traveling for the next seven days?"

Farrell sighed. Looking at the captivating redhead, he said, "Well, Mrs. Jordan, I guess you're going to have to stay put in that hotel after all."

Although the lawman was furious at the thought of Raven Morrow and Clete Hobbs getting away, there was nothing he could do about it. He was grateful at least that Marsha Burley had been witness to their plans. If nothing else, he knew where to head once he was able to travel again.

He looked up at Millie Jordan. It was obvious that she was even more fearful for Tommy—but all she could do now was pray.

Over the next two weeks, Raven Morrow and her gang crossed the state of Oregon and moved into Washington Territory, with November's cold wind and snow lashing them as they pressed northward. Raven now had fifteen in her outlaw band, having picked up new men, who had eagerly joined when the promise of gold was dangled in front of them. The gang robbed a trading post in a small settlement about twenty miles past the Oregon-Washington border, taking fur parkas, boots, gloves, and other supplies needed for enduring winter weather, and Maude Esther Dodd made sure Tommy Jordan was also provided for.

On the last day of November the gang robbed another trading post, this one at Spokane Falls, loading up on food, ammunition, whiskey, and tobacco. It was midafternoon when they beelined for the Canadian border, which was just under a hundred miles away.

As they plodded through ten inches of snow some two miles out of Spokane Falls, Bullard's eyes carefully surveyed the timber on a ridge about seventy yards to the left. Something had moved amid the lengthening shadows of the dense trees. Raven had not mentioned Tug Farrell for several days, but the marshal was never out of Bullard's thoughts. He had learned much about the man from Raven and Hobbs, and he was sure Farrell would show up sooner or later. Was that him up there in the timber? Something or somebody was up there, that was certain.

As the horses cut a path in the snow, blowing plumes of vapor from their nostrils, Bullard kept up a steady vigil to his left. Raven noticed it and, pulling her horse alongside Bullard's, she looked over Tommy's head and asked, "What are you watching, Jack?"

"Somethin' up there moved a minute ago. Caught my eye when it did, but then it moved back into the shadows. I'm waitin' for it to show itself again."

The attention of every person in the group was now on the ridge. Linus Meade spoke up. "Man or beast?"

"Couldn't tell."

Clete Hobbs pulled up on Bullard's other side. "You don't suppose it's Tug Farrell, do you?"

"Same thought crossed my mind," the huge bearded man answered.

Raven tensed and pulled her revolver, holding the muzzle to Tommy Jordan's head, which was covered by the hood of his parka. The boy's eyes widened with fear as she growled, "If it's Farrell, I'm ready for him."

Suddenly Bullard pulled rein. The others followed suit, straining to see whatever Jack had seen.

"What is it?" queried Raven, craning her neck and squinting against the lowering sun.

"Just keep your eyes on the spot where that fallen tree is," replied Bullard.

To a man, the gang began pulling rifles from saddle boots.

"Hold it!" Bullard snapped, lifting a gloved hand. "It's not Farrell."

Maude Esther Dodd gasped as a huge male timber wolf stepped from the shadows and looked straight at them.

Lester Jones, one of the new men, levered a cartridge into the chamber of his rifle and started to shoulder it.

"No!" commanded Bullard in a hoarse whisper. "Put that gun away!"

Suddenly a second form detached itself from the sunless gloom and flanked the first, and then a third emerged to stand abreast of the second. All three stood belly-deep in the snow and observed the group of riders, and the horses began whinnying and stomping nervously. There was additional movement in the shadows, then more wolves came out into the open, until nine could be counted.

Jack Bullard had been raised in the mountains of Montana and was well-acquainted with wolves' habits, temperament, and characteristics. He noted the gaunt look of the beasts, their ribs plainly visible under their dull coats. Apparently small game had been scarce in the area, and these wolves were extremely hungry— which could make them very dangerous.

"What should we do?" Raven asked.

"Just keep movin'," replied Bullard, nudging his horse into a walk.

The group pushed northward. The wary men kept their rifles ready, and to their left, staying within the timber, the wolves kept pace.

"Jack, you know about wolves," spoke up Raven. "Are we in for trouble?"

"Can't be sure," Bullard responded with a hint of hesitation. "It's obvious that this pack is hungry, and a gnawin' hunger can make any beast short-tempered. But normally wolves have a natural fear of humans and stay clear. I'd say probably there won't be any danger unless we provoke 'em."

"I know a man who was attacked by wolves, Jack,"

put in Mack Dugan. "He said they'd been short on food, but he did absolutely nothin' to provoke 'em."

"Did the man happen to be bleedin'?" queried Bullard.

Surprised at the question, Dugan answered, "Yeah. He was out in the woods cuttin' wood and whacked his hand. He was headin' through the forest for help when the wolves attacked. Lucky for him a couple of hunters were nearby and drove the wolves off with their rifles."

Nodding, Bullard explained that any carnivore was an opportunist. "They'll eat any carrion lyin' around, so naturally the smell of blood would attract 'em. If that critter was starvin', its first instinct was survival—overcomin' its fear of man and drivin' it to attack."

The wolf pack disappeared from sight after a while and had not reappeared by the time the gang pitched their tents and settled down for the night. Tommy Jordan slept next to Mack Dugan in Dugan's tent, telling the outlaw that he was terrified by the wolves.

Snickering, Dugan remarked, "Guess you better make sure you don't cut yourself then, kid. You'd sure make one tasty meal for one of them critters."

The boy huddled farther under his blanket, shaking with fear. He barely slept a wink all night, listening to the distant howling of the wolves.

When the gang awoke at dawn, the sky was heavy with leaden clouds, and the smell of snow was in the air, and as soon as breakfast was over, the gang packed up to move on. While Raven Morrow cinched the saddle on her horse, she remarked to Clete Hobbs and Jack Bullard, "I've been thinking about Farrell, and I'd say we were unnecessarily jumpy yesterday, expecting him to show. I figure something's happened to him, 'cause if he was coming, he certainly would have shown up by now." She gestured with her chin at Tommy Jordan, adding, "And that means we no longer need the brat."

Raven's words made the boy's blood freeze. He looked from Raven to Maude Esther Dodd standing nearby, silently asking for her help.

The portly woman walked closer, facing Raven and demanding, "Just what are you plannin' to do with him?"

Raven sneered and replied callously, "It's only about eight miles back to Spokane Falls. The brat can walk. Somebody there will take him in."

Maude Esther, looking bigger than ever in the thick parka that covered her blocky body, seemed to swell larger yet. She gestured toward the woods and bellowed, "Are you crazy? Those wolves are still out there! You heard 'em howlin' all night just like the rest of us did!"

Glaring at the larger woman, Raven snapped, "He's not bleeding, so the wolves won't bother him." Turning to the boy, she commanded, "Go on, kid! Get outta here!"

Maude Esther stepped directly in front of the brunette, her face inches away. "Have a heart, Raven! You can't make this boy walk back to Spokane Falls alone!"

Raven's eyes narrowed and her clipped words conveyed her anger. Her teeth bared, she growled, "Don't you tell me what I can and can't do, old woman!" She took a step toward Tommy Jordan and gave him a hard shove, knocking him into the snow. "I said get going! I'm sick of the sight of you!"

Maude Esther Dodd had clearly taken all she could stomach. With unexpected ferocity, she slapped Raven Morrow hard across the face, driving the smaller woman to her knees.

The gang members all stopped dead in their tracks.

Raven slowly stood up, and her rage was almost palpable. Breathing heavily through her nose, like a bull getting ready to charge, she stood glaring at Maude Esther. Then, swearing vehemently, she reached for her revolver. But the older woman showed surprising agility, and she leapt at Raven and grabbed her wrist, making it impossible for the brunette to fire.

Screaming with fury, Raven struggled to free her wrist. Suddenly the big woman released her grip and chopped the smaller woman on the jaw with a meaty

fist. Raven's feet left the ground and she landed on her
back in the snow, then thrashed about, trying to get up.

Seeming even more than ever like a protective
mother bear, what with her fur parka, the Dodd woman
leapt onto Raven and pounded her with both fists.
Raven tried to fight back, but the bigger woman was too
strong, and Maude Esther began to take control.

The older woman finally let go of her adversary and
got to her feet, breathing hard. "Had enough, you evil
witch?" she gasped, her fists balled and ready. "Or do
you want more?"

Raven struggled to her feet, holding her arms out
in supplication, when Jack Bullard suddenly tossed a
knife into her right hand. Raven instantly lunged at the
buxom woman, swinging the deadly blade, and, taken
by surprise, Maude Esther was unable to dodge it. Cold
steel stabbed through the parka, puncturing the woman's upper arm and coming out the other side. Eyes
wild, and smiling victoriously, Raven jerked the knife
free.

Maude Esther grabbed her wounded arm and
stumbled to her knees. Blood was seeping through the
slits in the sleeve of the parka. Tommy ran to her, crying, "Maude Esther! You're bleeding!"

Raven gave Bullard his bloody knife, which he
wiped off in the snow. Then Clete Hobbs handed her
the revolver and, brushing snow from the gun, she
cocked it and pointed it at the bleeding woman, barking, "Get going, woman, and take that brat with you!"
When Maude Esther put her arm around Tommy and
started toward her horse, Raven screamed, "On foot!"

The pair slowly turned and started trudging
through the snow toward the south.

When they were fifty yards away, one of the new
men stepped up to Raven and angrily told her, "You've
just sent that woman and boy to their deaths! Those
starvin' wolves will smell her blood and attack!"

Raven Morrow bristled. "Do you think I'm stupid?"
she retorted. "I passed up the pleasure of watching her
die in front of me for the sweet thought of her being

torn to shreds!" Scowling, she added in a steely voice,
"But you don't have to worry about them, Mr. Jones."
As she spoke, Raven whipped out her gun and without
warning shot the man in the stomach. He buckled,
clutched the wound, and fell, a shocked expression on
his face. "I'm not accustomed to being spoken to in such
a manner, Mr. Jones," she hissed. "Too bad you didn't
learn that." The other men looked on in silence as
Raven cocked her gun again and stood over the gutshot
outlaw. He looked up, gasping, his eyes focused on the
black bore pointed between his eyes. "Consider this
your final lesson." She squeezed the trigger, and Lester
Jones died as the slug tore into his skull.

Snow was beginning to fall as Maude Esther and
Tommy Jordan started away from camp. When they
heard the shots, they stopped and looked back. They
watched the gang mount up and pull out, taking two
riderless horses with them. Raven and her men were no
more than forty yards from the campsite when the
wolves darted from the timber and began to devour
Lester Jones's body.

Gripping her wounded arm, which was leaving a
trail of blood on the freshly fallen snow, Maude Esther
told the boy, "Tommy, we've got to run for town as fast
as we can! When the wolves are through with that body,
they'll be after us!"

They ran for their lives, and after covering over six
miles, they could see Spokane Falls in the distance.
Their legs weary and their lungs feeling as though they
were on fire, the pair stopped to rest a moment. Tommy
looked back and gasped. "Maude Esther! The wolf pack
is coming!"

Her strength was spent and, still losing blood,
Maude Esther Dodd knew her death was inevitable.
"Tommy," she panted, "I can't make it. You run! I'll
distract the wolves away from you."

Terror was on the boy's face. "But, Maude Esther—"

"Don't argue with me, Tommy!" she begged. "Go!"

Sobbing, the ten-year-old boy pivoted and headed for Spokane Falls with all his might. When he had gone a hundred yards, he stopped, panting for breath, and looked back. Maude Esther Dodd was down in the snow, screaming horribly and thrashing about as the wolves ripped and tore at her flesh.

Half-blinded by scalding tears, the redheaded boy turned and forced his exhausted body on to Spokane Falls.

# Chapter Thirteen

At Burney, California, U.S. Marshal Tug Farrell was ready to travel after three weeks of recuperation. Millie Jordan and he had been occupying separate rooms in the town's only hotel. They had spent a good deal of time together, and although neither one had shown it, they were feeling a strong attraction for each other.

At dawn on the day they were to resume travel, Farrell was shaving in his hotel room, thinking of the beautiful redhead, and that, despite the danger, he was glad she would be traveling with him. He was just finishing his task, shaving carefully around his mustache, when there was a knock at the door, and he smiled, glad that Millie was so prompt. Laying the straight razor on the washstand, he wiped his face with a towel and limped to the door. When he turned the knob, the door whipped open, slamming him to the floor. Stunned, Farrell looked up to see Vic Devlin standing over him with a gun in his hand.

Regarding the lawman with his single wicked eye, a black patch over the blinded one, the outlaw kicked the door shut. "I shot your old man right between the eyes," hissed the killer. "Now I'm gonna shoot out both of yours."

Furious at the contempt the man showed toward his father, the marshal kicked Devlin's legs out from under him. Instantly they were wrestling on the floor, with the outlaw trying to turn his gun on the man he had come to kill. They slammed into the bed, then rose to their feet, matching each other in both strength and determination. Farrell's wounded leg was hurting, but he ignored the pain. Bracing his feet, he mustered all the strength he could into his left hand, jerking Devlin's wrist violently. The revolver sailed across the room and crashed out the window.

Devlin swore and tried to get a choke hold on the marshal. Farrell was spun around in the struggle, and his wounded thigh slammed into the dresser. Pain lanced through him. He glanced down and saw blood soaking through his pants, and it was as if the sight of the blood renewed his resolve.

He broke a hand free and punched Devlin solidly, knocking him across the room. Devlin got up, and the marshal limped toward him to finish the fight, but he was unsteady on his feet. The outlaw sidestepped him and kicked the wounded leg savagely, and Farrell gasped, then dropped to one knee.

Vic Devlin looked around the room, then grinned. He staggered toward Farrell's gun belt hanging on the bedpost at the head of the bed. Watching him, the lawman knew that he was dead if the killer made it to the gun, and in spite of the agonizing pain, he sprang up and grabbed his straight razor on the washstand. In a desperate fight for life, he tackled Devlin before the man reached the gun, and, rolling him over, slashed him across the throat. With his jugular veins oozing blood, the outlaw managed to scramble to his feet, screaming, and head for the door, clutching at his throat to stay the flow of blood. Devlin had taken only a few steps when his blood and his life ran out, and he collapsed. Then a black curtain descended over Farrell as he passed out.

When U.S. Marshal Tug Farrell opened his eyes, he looked into the face of Dr. Jeremiah Winslow. "Welcome back," the elderly physician said with a smile. "In case you're wondering, you're on my operating table, and I've just restitched and bandaged that wound of yours."

"Devlin?" groaned the marshal.

"That the fella you were fighting?"

"Yes."

"Died before I got to the hotel. Bled to death."

Farrell nodded, feeling a degree of satisfaction. He had at least avenged his father's murder.

"How did I get here?"

"Well, the hotel clerk heard a ruckus in your room and called the town marshal. He went up and found the two of you, then called me."

At that moment, the door burst open and Millie Jordan hurried to Farrell's side. Taking hold of his hand, she looked down at him with worried eyes and said, "I was just notified about you, Tug. Was it Vic Devlin?"

"Yes."

"So you were right. You must have said a dozen times you thought he'd find a way to break jail and come after you."

"Well, it's over now," the lawman declared with a sigh.

Tears filled Millie's eyes. Squeezing his hand tighter, she sniffed and murmured, "Oh, I'm so glad you're all right! I was so worried about you, darling!"

Farrell smiled crookedly. "I didn't think my hearing was damaged at all in that fight, but I could have sworn you just called me darling."

Millie Jordan blushed furiously.

Clearing his throat noisily, Dr. Jeremiah Winslow murmured that he needed to take care of something in the outer office, and quickly excused himself.

Millie watched him go, and when the door shut, she leaned down close and breathed, "Dr. Winslow is very tactful—and, yes, you heard right. I did call you darling."

Grinning broadly, the lawman asked, "Are you admitting what I should have admitted by now myself?"

"Mm-hmm." She laughed, then bent her head to his and kissed him. Placing a hand on the back of her head, Farrell pressed her tighter to him, and their first kiss was a lingering one.

* * *

After five more days, Tug Farrell was once again ready to travel, and he and Millie finally left Burney. They moved north through increasingly colder weather and snow, asking questions of people along the way. With the seasoned lawman's nose for tracking, they followed the gang's trail across Oregon and into Washington. Winter storms slowed them some, but they pushed on in spite of the weather, and one snowy evening in late December they arrived in Spokane Falls.

They looked around for a place to stay and a place to eat, but there was no hotel, and there were no cafés. There was a large trading post, but it was closed.

"Not much more than a settlement here," the lawman commented. "Maybe we can find some hospitable folks who'll take us in for the night and feed us."

At that moment an old man appeared, walking from one side of the broad street to the other. "Excuse me, sir," called Farrell.

The old man stopped and eyed the two riders from under the brim of a tattered hat.

The lawman introduced himself and Millie, telling the man, "We've been traveling all day, sir, and we were hoping there'd be a place to stay here, but I don't see a hotel. Would you happen to know if there might be someone who could put us up for the night? We'd be glad to pay."

The oldster's eyes lit up. "By some chance, is your wife expecting a baby, mister?"

Farrell and Millie exchanged puzzled glances; then the marshal answered, "No, she isn't, sir. As a matter of fact, the lady isn't my wife, either."

Waving a gloved hand through the air, the wrinkled old man exclaimed, "Aw, shucks! I thought maybe it'd be almost like it was on that night a couple thousand years ago. You know . . ."

Millie suddenly smiled, understanding the reference. "Are you talking about the first Christmas?" she asked.

"Yes'm!" He peered at her sharply. "Don't you know this is Christmas Eve?"

Farrell and Millie looked at each other in utter surprise; then Millie explained, "We've been traveling a long time, sir. All the way from Sacramento, California. And we completely lost track of the date."

Stepping closer to the travelers, the old man smiled and said, "My name's Hezekiah Westlake. M'friends call me Hezzy. I've got a two-room shack over there a ways. It ain't much, but there's a feather bed in the bedroom and a creaky ol' couch in the main room . . . and plenty of floor space. You can sleep in the feather bed, ma'am. Us fellas can fight over the sofa. Loser has to spend the night on the floor. I was about to go home and heat up some grub. If that sounds okay to the two of you, you're welcome to spend Christmas Eve with me."

They gladly accepted the old man's generosity, offering to pay him whatever he wished, but he would have nothing of it, telling them he was happy to have a genuine U.S. marshal in his humble home—not to mention such a beautiful lady, he added, smiling at Millie. While the meal was cooking, Farrell and Millie began filling the old bachelor in on their story. They had gotten halfway through the meal by the time the story was complete, and Hezzy had fallen strangely quiet.

When the meal was finished, Farrell and Millie insisted on doing the cleaning up, and while they were washing the dishes with melted snow, the oldster slid into his overcoat and hobbled to the door. Donning his hat, he grinned and declared, "The way you two look at each other, I'd say you done fell in love on this trip. You can do a little smoochin' while I'm gone. I'll be back shortly."

"Where are you going?" the redhead asked. "I hope you aren't leaving on our account."

"Well, in a manner of speaking," he answered. Millie immediately protested, but he held up his hand. "It's Christmas Eve, ain't it?"

"Yes."

"Well, I thought of a little Christmas present I want to get you."

Millie started to ask the old man not to do such a thing, but he was out and gone too quickly. Shrugging, she went back to her task.

As soon as Farrell and Millie were done, they sat in front of the potbellied stove and did indeed embrace and kiss several times. Millie held the lawman's hand, lamenting that she hated not being with her son on Christmas and wondering if he, too, had forgotten what day it was.

Her chin began to quiver, when suddenly feet were heard stamping snow from boots on the porch. Composing herself, she turned to the door as it swung open, but instead of Hezekiah Westlake appearing in the doorway, there stood a redheaded boy in a parka. Millie Jordan gave a cry of unbridled joy. Releasing Farrell's hand, she clambered to her feet and rushed to her son, hugging him tight. Both of them burst into tears as they embraced, and Millie pulled the hood off Tommy's head and showered him with kisses. The lawman stood looking on, smiling broadly and fighting the hot lump that insisted on rising in his throat.

While holding her boy, Millie smiled through tear-filled eyes at the old man, giving him a look of gratitude, and then she knelt and gazed almost disbelievingly into the face of her son. With tears streaming down her cheeks, she declared, "This is my happiest Christmas ever! But tell me, how did this happen? How did you get away from that awful woman?"

Between the boy and the old man, Farrell and Millie were filled in on the details. They learned of Maude Esther Dodd's fight with Raven Morrow and of her sacrificial death to keep the wolves from attacking Tommy. When the boy had appeared in Spokane Falls over three weeks ago, a young couple took him into their home, planning to return him to his home in Sacramento come the spring thaw. In the meantime, they sent a wire to the boy's home, but in his mother's absence, no one had been there to receive it.

Hearing of Raven Morrow's ruthless and brutal treatment of the woman and the boy, Tug Farrell renewed his vow to bring her and her heartless gang to justice.

Keeping one arm around Tommy, Millie then took Tug Farrell's hand and introduced them, explaining Farrell's mission and his promise to rescue Tommy. She also told the boy about Farrell's thigh wound, telling him why they had been so long in coming.

There was appreciation in young Tommy's eyes as he stepped forward and offered his small hand to the towering marshal. "I'm very glad to meet you, sir," he said with feeling. "Thank you for taking care of Mom . . . and for coming to rescue me." Then the boy confided, "I heard Raven and Clete Hobbs talk about you a lot. They really hate you. Especially her."

"That's hardly surprising," he said dryly.

Tommy then looked from his mother to the lawman, cocked his head, and asked, "Marshal Farrell, are you going to be my new dad?"

Farrell was nonplussed. Blushing, he glanced at Millie, and her face was the same color. "Why do you ask that?"

"'Cause you hold hands a lot. When I came in, you were holding hands, and now you're doing it again."

Millie suddenly giggled and wrapped both arms around her son, declaring, "Why is it that children always say things adults only think?"

She quickly changed the subject, telling Hezzy that she wanted to thank the young couple who had cared for Tommy.

"And so you shall," the old man responded. "In the mornin'. Right now it's time these old bones went to sleep—and the three of you better get a good rest, too. You've got a lot of travelin' ahead of you."

Early the next morning, the four of them stepped out into the cold and headed across town. Reaching the house of the couple who had sheltered Tommy, Tug Farrell announced that he was going after the gang alone. Learning of the lawman's quest, the young couple insisted that Millie and Tommy stay with them until the marshal could return and escort them home.

Turning to the old man, Farrell asked, "Would you mind having my company for a couple of days more, Hezzy? Now that we know Tommy's safe, I wouldn't mind resting my leg for a bit—especially since I know exactly where Raven and her bunch are heading."

"It's fine with me," Hezzy declared expansively.

Two days later, U.S. Marshal Tug Farrell, wearing a new buffalo-hide coat he had purchased at the trading post, dismounted in front of the young couple's home and walked to the porch. Millie answered his knock, explaining that the couple were in town getting some stores. Farrell smiled down at the boy, then, ruffling his hair, ordered, "Take good care of your mother while I'm gone, son."

The redheaded, freckle-faced boy looked up at Farrell with admiring eyes and assured him, "Don't worry, I will." The lawman then took Millie in his arms and kissed her. He was still holding her when Tommy asked again, "Are you going to be my new dad?"

Farrell paused, looked lovingly into Millie's eyes, and replied, "Why don't you and your mother talk about it while I'm gone?"

Millie leaned away from him and gave him a sidelong look. "There's nothing to talk about. I've had no proposal."

The beautiful woman was suddenly wrapped in powerful arms, then kissed again with even more feeling. When their lips parted, Farrell announced, "Well, you've got one now!"

"There's still nothing for Tommy and me to talk about," she remarked offhandedly.

Farrell arched his eyebrows. "Oh?"

Running her fingers through Tommy's hair, Millie shrugged and grinned, explaining, "I already know what Tommy wants, and I want the same thing. Tommy and I will be waiting for you, *Dad!*"

By the last week of December, Raven Morrow had picked up another man to replace Lester Jones, and she and her fourteen men were running their own mine in the Selkirk Mountains of British Columbia, having murdered the men who had been in charge. Situated in a snow-covered draw, the site was surrounded on three sides by heavily timbered hills, while the mouth was in the rock face of a huge mountain. Raven had her own cabin in the draw, and the men lived in shacks. Come spring, they would start kidnapping men for slave labor.

On January 12, 1878, U.S. Marshal Tug Farrell crossed the Canadian border just south of the town of Trail. At the border station he encountered two members of the Royal Canadian Mounted Police, who since 1873 had been protecting the people of their country. Farrell explained his mission to the two mounties, giving the approximate location of the Selkirk mines, which Tommy Jordan had related to him from overhearing many conversations between Raven Morrow and her men.

One of the mounties told the lawman, "We would like to help you, Marshal, but we have to remain here on duty."

Smiling ironically, Farrell told them, "That's okay, gentlemen. This is *my* fight!"

It took three days of riding through the deep snow, checking out various mining camps, before the determined lawman found the right one. Then, hiding in the timber on a steep hillside above Raven's camp, Farrell huddled against the subzero cold in his buffalo-hide coat and observed the activity below. After a full day of watching, he knew that Raven lived in the cabin alone and that she had thirteen men in addition to Clete Hobbs.

As he thought of the death-strewn trail left behind them and of how they were willing to let a helpless, innocent child face a pack of starving wolves, Farrell's blood heated up. Grinding his teeth, he said to himself, "Okay, Raven Morrow, Tug Farrell has just declared war!"

# Chapter Fourteen

At sunup the next morning, U.S. Marshal Tug Farrell, armed with his revolver, a big knife, and a .44-caliber Winchester seven-shot repeater, leaned against a snow-laden pine tree high above the camp, watching for movement below. Squinting against the glare of the rising sun, he suddenly stiffened as the doors to the shacks started opening and Raven's men stepped outside into the bone-chilling twenty-below-zero air. They ran with their heads down, the stiff wind blowing off the mountain whipping them as they dashed across the open expanse of the compound to the mine entrance.

Farrell had noticed the day before that Clete Hobbs shared a shack with a huge bearded man, but so far neither of them had appeared—nor had Raven Morrow emerged from her cabin. It seemed to be both Hobbs's and the other man's routine to go in and out of the mine often during the day, and the lawman planned to wait until the two of them were down in the mine before breaking into Raven's cabin. Catching her off guard, he would bind and gag her, then wait for one of Hobbs's frequent trips from the mine and grab him. With the gang leaders securely out of commission, Farrell would be free to figure a way to take the rest of the men. He felt it was important for Raven and Hobbs to stay alive so they would die on the gallows in Denver, but he did not see how he could manage to capture all the others. Though he would gladly take prisoners as an alternative to killing, there would probably be no choice but to shoot it out with Raven's gang.

Swinging his arms and stomping his feet to stay warm, Tug Farrell counted the twelfth man to enter the mine. That left only Hobbs and the bearded man. Deciding he could wait no longer, the marshal descended into the draw. He would move in on the woman, then go for Hobbs and his huge crony.

Rifle cocked and ready, Farrell dashed across the snow-covered draw, weaving among the shacks, and drew up to a side wall of Raven's cabin. He inched up to a window but could not see inside, for the window was thick with ice. Looking about to make sure no one was in sight, he rounded the corner of the small building, leapt onto the porch, then hit the door hard with his shoulder. It sprang open onto an empty room. Raven was not there.

Swearing under his breath, he turned and looked cautiously out the door, checking carefully all around the compound. No one was in sight, and he made a run for Clete Hobbs's shack, again thundering in after hitting the door hard. That shack was empty as well. Stumped, he wondered where and when Raven and the two men had gone. Suddenly he heard voices outside. Stepping cautiously to the open doorway, he peered around the frame. He took a step out of Hobbs's shack just as three gang members emerged from the mine and saw him.

One of the men pointed at him, shouting, "Ain't no way Clete and them's back from the tradin' post yet! Seems to me we have a visitor!"

The three men pulled their revolvers and darted toward the shack. Wanting to take them alive, Farrell leveled his rifle and ordered, "Hold it right there! I'm a U.S. marshal! Drop those guns!"

Ignoring him, they immediately brought their guns up for action. Farrell's rifle barked, its report echoing through the draw. The man to Farrell's right took the slug in his chest, its impact flattening him to his back. Quickly levering another shell into the chamber, the marshal fired and the next man went down, shot in the head. Before the lawman had the chance to shoot the third man, the outlaw fired, but his bullet whirred past Farrell's head, boring into the shack behind him. The marshal's return slug was deadly accurate.

Four more gang members materialized from the black mouth of the mine several yards behind the three forms sprawled in the snow. Farrell sprinted around the back of Hobbs's shack as the foursome opened fire, their bullets chewing wood where Farrell had been standing seconds before. Working the lever on his rifle, the lawman moved to the opposite corner of the shack and took aim at a man heading for the cover of a supply building near the mouth of the mine. The shell missed the man as he dived to safety, while the three others bellied down in the snow and unleashed a barrage at Farrell.

The marshal knew that if the rest of the gang were anywhere near the surface of the mine, they would definitely hear the gunfire. He had to work fast.

Suddenly one of the three in the snow jumped up and ran a few feet, shooting as he went, then bellied down again. Farrell aimed, fired, and the man let out a scream. His body jerked spasmodically for a few seconds as his blood turned the white snow around him red.

One of the others then leapt up and zigzagged toward the shack. Lining up the rifle muzzle on him, Farrell squeezed the trigger, hitting the man in the shoulder. The outlaw went down but then raised his gun to shoot back. Farrell was about to shoot him again when the man behind the supply shack started firing. The third man then jumped to his feet, and Farrell darted back behind the shack for cover and ran to the opposite end. Breathing hard, Farrell realized they would try to get him in a cross fire. But just as the one outlaw reached the corner of the shack to step around and gun the lawman down, Farrell met him and pulled the trigger of the rifle. The slug ripped into the outlaw's throat, and he went down like a tree felled by a woodsman's ax.

Farrell wheeled and returned to where he had been. Peering around carefully, he saw the wounded man heading toward him, ready to shoot. The marshal lined the gun on the man and fired, but the hammer struck an empty chamber. Not having time to reload, he dropped the rifle and pulled out his revolver; then, aiming at the wounded man, he shot him in the head. From the corner of his eye he caught sight of the last man leaving the cover of the supply shack, heading for the dark mouth of the mine—obviously going after reinforcements.

Raising his left arm, the marshal laid the barrel of the Colt .45 on it to steady his aim, then squeezed off the shot. The man took the bullet high on the left side, dropped his gun, and fell facedown in the snow some thirty feet from the entrance to the mine.

Farrell knew there were five more men in the mine. He had been mighty lucky so far with the first seven and in escaping injury himself. Could his luck hold out with the last five? He suddenly had an idea. Picking up his empty rifle while holding the Colt in his other hand, he made a run for the supply shack. He knew that all miners had to use dynamite periodically to remove large sections of rock—and that dynamite might well be the key to survival for Tug Farrell.

While dashing across the compound, he kept his eyes glued on the mine entrance. No one emerged. He hurriedly knelt down and rifled the pockets of one of the dead outlaws, finding some matches. He was almost at the supply shack when the man he had shot near the mine's mouth struggled to his feet and staggered into the dark maw. Farrell knew that if the outlaw did not collapse before he reached the men who were apparently deeper in the mine, there soon would be five more guns to contend with.

Reaching the supply shack, Farrell plunged inside. Sure enough, there were several boxes of dynamite stacked up, and the one on top was open, exposing the

red cylinders with their snakelike fuses. Suddenly loud,
excited voices came from the mouth of the mine, and it
was obvious that the wounded man had reached his
cohorts. Grabbing four of the deadly sticks, Farrell
pulled out his knife and shortened the fuses on them.
He then removed his gloves, put several matches between his lips, and stepped outside, holding the four
sticks in his left hand and his revolver in his right. Two
men were emerging from the dark shadows, carrying
their revolvers. Farrell fired at them three times, and
they darted back into the mine. Holstering his gun, the
lawman flared a match with a thumbnail and lit one of
the short fuses. It began sizzling.

One of the outlaws appeared again, raising his gun.
Farrell leapt aside, dodging the bullet, and tossed the
sparking stick of dynamite straight at the man. He
screamed just before it hit him in the chest and exploded, blowing his body to pieces. The man behind
him also screamed and was then blown apart.

There was no time to waste, and Farrell quickly lit
the remaining sticks of dynamite. Thundering shouts
echoed from inside the mine as the rest of the outlaws
raced for the mouth. The marshal tossed the three sticks
into the dark opening, then wheeled and ran a few
yards before diving to the snow-covered ground and
lying flat, his hands over his head.

A moment's ominous hush was then punctured by
hysterical voices within the mine; then thunder rocked
the mountain as the three sticks of dynamite exploded
in a trio of rapid, booming concussions. When all was
again quiet, the marshal stood up, his ears ringing.
Brushing the snow off the buffalo-hide coat, he stared at
what had been the mouth of the mine. It was now filled
with dirt and broken rock, and dust wafted into the
frigid air as though pushed by a giant bellows.

Returning to the shelter of the supply shack, the
marshal reloaded his Winchester and his Colt .45.
"Okay, Raven," he breathed, dropping the Colt in its
holster, "I'm ready for you and your two friends. Come
on back, and let's get this over with."

It was obvious that Raven Morrow and the two men had left before sunrise, so he had not witnessed their departure. Closing the door of the supply shack, U.S. Marshal Tug Farrell sat down on a wooden box and waited. A wide crack in the wall that faced the cabin and shacks gave him a clear view of the trail leading into the draw. He would be able to see the outlaws when they rode in.

While waiting, the big man thought of Millie Jordan and her bright-eyed son. He felt incredibly fortunate that such a wonderful and beautiful woman had fallen in love with him. And Tommy . . . What man could ask for a better son? The rugged lawman was eager to get back to them.

Suddenly he saw movement through the crack. Focusing, he saw three riders coming down the wooded hillside into the draw. They were still some distance away, but Farrell could pick out the bulk of the huge bearded man.

Hurrying out of the supply shack, the marshal dashed around back and climbed up the hill into the trees at the far end of the draw. Hunkering low, he watched as Raven Morrow, Clete Hobbs, and the big man rode closer.

Suddenly Raven saw the bodies strewn about and her voice echoed across the compound in a string of profanity. She swore again when she turned her head and saw the rubble that filled the mouth of the mine.

All three leapt from their saddles, drawing their guns and looking about warily. Farrell was crouching about forty feet from where they stood. Looking over, he could see Raven's face flush with anger under the hood of her parka as she shouted at the two men, "It's *Farrell*! I know it!" Walking around in a tight circle, she bellowed, "Farrell! Farrell! Come on out and fight like a man!" The words bounced off the high hills, repeating again and again.

Jack Bullard ran his gaze over the surrounding forest and advised, "We'd better take cover. He could pick us off easily where we stand."

"That's not his style, Jack," Raven retorted, her voice raised in anger. "The man won't pick us off from ambush."

"Oh, yeah? Then what'd he do with all these guys?" asked Bullard sarcastically, gesturing at all the corpses stiffening in the snow.

"I'll guarantee you he gave them a chance to surrender," Clete Hobbs answered. "He wears a badge, remember?"

"What are we gonna do?" asked Bullard.

"We're going to find him and kill him," Raven responded flatly. "He's either up there among those trees, or he's hiding in my cabin or one of the shacks. Jack, you climb up onto the hillside at this end and work your way over, and, Clete, you go up at the other end. It's plain to see he isn't anywhere on the face of that big mountain. I'll search the buildings. First one sees him, cut loose with your guns and the other two of us will come running. This is Tug Farrell's day to die—and I want it to happen sooner rather than later. Let's go."

Overhearing the plan, Tug Farrell decided to follow the man named Jack Bullard and take him out first. The marshal waited until Raven was inside a shack and Clete Hobbs had disappeared toward the south; then, weaving among the trees, he sprinted rapidly toward the huge bearded man. With his gun held out in front of him, ready to fire, Bullard climbed steadily higher, and soon the camp below was out of sight. The marshal was to the side of him as the outlaw crested the high hill, then walked away from Farrell along the edge. The lawman followed at a slight distance, and soon the huge man reached the sheer face of the mountain and could go no farther. Swearing, he turned to head back.

Farrell stood there, holding his gun on Bullard. "Looking for me?" asked the marshal, his breath visible in the subzero air.

Bullard merely stared at the lawman with loathing.

"Drop your gun. Now," the marshal commanded sharply.

Challenge leapt into Jack Bullard's eyes. "And if I don't?"

Farrell started to reply, but it was cut short by Bullard bringing his gun up. Having no choice, the marshal fired, and his Colt roared. The bullet struck the huge man in the chest, staggering him, but instead of falling, he raised the gun again. The lawman fired a second time, but though the bearded man dropped to his knees, he would not relinquish his gun.

Amazed that the man could take two .45 slugs and still be alive, Farrell ran to him and jerked the revolver from his hand. But as he did so, the massive man lunged at Farrell, knocking him down. Before the marshal could recover, the gun was torn from his own hand and Bullard was on top of him, his huge hands wrapped around the marshal's throat and the thumbs pressing hard on his Adam's apple.

Despite two slugs in him, the man had the power of a bull and Farrell could not get free. The lawman's eyes were bulging from their sockets, his face was turning purple, and it felt as though his windpipe were being crushed. Struggling to maintain his consciousness, Farrell reached under the heavy buffalo-hide coat and his hand closed on the hasp of his knife. Summoning all his strength, he pulled out the knife and drove the twelve-inch blade into Jack Bullard's right side. The giant howled but kept pressing down on the marshal's windpipe. Farrell managed to yank the knife out and plunge it in again, and Bullard's hands finally relaxed against the marshal's throat. The lawman stabbed Bullard twice more to make sure the man was done for.

Bullard's hulk plopped lifelessly on top of the marshal. Wriggling free, Tug Farrell crawled away from the man, then struggled to his feet, gagging and sucking hard for air while clutching his throat. He spied his Colt .45 in the snow where Bullard had thrown it, but just as he bent to pick it up, a gunshot cracked from behind him, and he felt the bullet sear into his left thigh. Dropping into the snow, he palmed the .45, rolled over, and found his target as Clete Hobbs was about to fire again.

The gun in Farrell's hand roared and Hobbs took the slug square in the chest as his own gun fired again. The bullet chopped the bark from a tree near Farrell's shoulder, and the weapon slipped from Hobbs's fingers. He staggered for a moment, calling Farrell a vile name, then fell facedown in the snow.

Quickly Farrell examined the wound. The bullet had gone all the way through his leg this time, but it was within an inch of where he had been hit before.

Knowing the gunshots would bring Raven Morrow, the wounded lawman limped through the brush to where he had climbed up from the draw. Leaning his rifle against a tree, Farrell opened the big coat and pulled out his shirttail, then ripped off a large piece. He limped over to a boulder and leaned against it, about to wrap the makeshift bandage around the bleeding leg.

His heart almost stopped when he heard a low growl behind him. Turning slowly, he found himself face-to-face with an enormous timber wolf, its ribs sticking out of its gaunt body. Its snout was wrinkled back in a vicious snarl, and it was obviously ready to pounce.

Farrell's rifle was too far away for him to reach, and the buffalo-hide coat covered his holster, preventing a quick draw. The knife was in its sheath on his left side, and it would take even longer to get it out.

While the thoughts were still flashing through his mind, the starving wolf lunged, and Farrell collapsed under the thrust of the animal's weight. The horrendous pain in his leg was quickly forgotten as he desperately fought off the lashing, snarling fangs of a beast desperate to survive.

The lawman's adrenaline racing, he managed to ram an elbow to the side of the wolf's head and stun it momentarily. Farrell scrambled to his knees and reached under the heavy coat for his revolver, but he was too slow. The animal was on him again before he could get a grip on the butt of the gun, and its fangs slashed the buffalo-hide coat, trying to get at Farrell's throat.

The marshal rolled in the snow, kicking and slam-

ming punches at the animal. Suddenly the two of them
peeled over the edge of the gully and tumbled through
the snow all the way to the bottom. They came to a stop
a few feet apart, and while the wolf was struggling to its
feet, the marshal opened the coat and clawed for his
revolver. He got it out of the holster, but before he
could bring it to bear, the wolf sprang. The snapping
fangs tore at his wrist and the Colt fell into the snow.

Again, man and beast were in a death struggle,
thrashing about in the snow. Farrell used his arms and
elbows to fend off the fangs, but the wolf's immensely
strong jaws easily tore gashes in the thick hide of the
coat and slashed the lawman's flesh. At one point, they
slammed into a fallen tree, and the beast cracked its
head against the log, yelping in pain and becoming
momentarily dazed.

Leaping to his feet, the lawman gasped for breath.
He knew he could not last much longer, for his leg,
throbbing with pain, was bleeding profusely, and his
strength was waning. Farrell suddenly noticed a thick
broken limb hanging by a piece of bark just above his
head. Grabbing it, he ripped it loose just as the wolf
lunged at him again, growling and snapping. Using the
limb as a club, Farrell swung it violently against the
wolf's head. The wood connected with bone with a loud
crack, and the wolf collapsed in a heap in the snow and
lay still.

Gulping the frigid air that burned his lungs, Farrell
staggered about, looking for his Colt, but it was buried
somewhere in the snow, nowhere to be found. The
lawman could tell his face was scratched and cut, and he
knelt down and rubbed snow all over it. He threw a last
glance at the wolf, lying in the snow, unmoving, and
started the climb back up to the rim of the gully. Bleeding and exhausted, he struggled through the snow, falling several times, but he pushed himself on. Raven
would be showing up soon, and he had to get his rifle.

Farrell staggered toward the spot where his rifle
leaned against the fallen tree, but never made it. Everything began to whirl around him, and he fell to the

ground. He shook his head to clear it, but it was to no avail, and he blacked out.

Coming to, U.S. Marshal Tug Farrell opened his eyes and stared at the waving treetops overhead. He was lying on his back in the snow, and the wind was whipping icy particles against him. He was cold . . . *very* cold. Suddenly he realized that his coat was gone. Rising on an elbow, he saw that his knife was missing from its sheath. Then he heard a diabolical laugh as Raven Morrow stepped into his line of sight. A dozen feet away, she was holding his rifle and wearing the big buffalo-hide coat, which reached down to her ankles. Her black eyes, wicked and vitriolic, were pinned on Farrell, and he felt as though the devil himself was looking at him.

"So!" Raven declared, sneering at him. "You killed all my men—but from the looks of those cuts and scratches on your face, at least Jack gave you a good fight, lawman. But if you think little Raven is whipped, you've got another guess coming. There are plenty more men out there who'll help me, Farrell, and I intend to be the richest woman in the world someday." She snorted. "You just won't be around to see it."

The marshal struggled to a sitting position. His left pant leg was stiff with frozen blood. He looked at the rifle she held, then raised his eyes to her face once more.

Raven knew what he was thinking. Throwing her head back and laughing wickedly, she said, "No such luck, lawman. I *was* going to put a bullet through your head, but I changed my mind. I think you need to die real slow. Which do you think it will be? Will you bleed to death . . . or freeze to death? I can't wait to find out —and I'm going to wait right here and watch."

Farrell shifted his eyes when he caught movement behind her. The wolf Farrell had clubbed to insensibility was stalking toward them, its maddened eyes focused on Raven Morrow and smelling on the buffalo-hide coat Farrell's scent—the man who had injured it earlier. A low growl came from its throat. Raven turned her head then, but before either she or Farrell could react, the wolf lunged.

The beast leapt onto her, sinking its fangs into her throat. Dropping Farrell's rifle, she screamed and clawed at the snarling, snapping animal. "Help me!" she shrieked as she wrestled the wolf. "Farrell! Help me!"

Rolling to his knees, Farrell crawled toward the rifle lying in the snow a few yards distant, but he managed only a couple of feet before he fell flat. His body was so cold, he could barely function.

The wolf's snarls spiraled into a higher pitch as it ripped and tore at Raven while she fought furiously for her life. Blood was spurting from her throat where the slashing teeth had torn through the skin, and her cries were barely audible. The beast pinned her to the ground and stood over her with its slavering jaws snapping viciously at her face.

She managed a scream as the wolf lifted its face from hers momentarily, spraying her with bloody saliva. Farrell watched in horror as she desperately held her hands over her face, trying to protect herself from the deadly fangs, and first her fingers were torn to shreds, then her hands were mangled.

Pushing himself beyond his limit, Farrell finally managed to reach the rifle. Gaining his feet, he aimed at the animal, whose face, mouth, and coat were covered with blood. It turned and glared at this new adversary and, leaving the woman, lunged for the lawman, fangs bared. Farrell squeezed the trigger and the bullet entered the animal's open mouth, blowing its brains out the back of its head. It collapsed in the snow a few feet from its mauled victim.

The raw wind whipped across the snow-covered hills and bit into Tug Farrell's body like a knife. Steeling himself, he staggered over to Raven Morrow, who looked up at him with glassy eyes. The last breath left her, and then she lay still, staring up vacantly at the winter sky.

Farrell pulled the heavy buffalo-hide coat off her,

then shouldered into it. Immediately his body began to regain its warmth.

The big man stumbled and groped his way toward where he had left his horse sheltered in a stand of pines. Passing Jack Bullard's body on the way, he used the dead man's shirt as a fresh bandage for his wound. Thankfully the brutally cold air had almost stopped the bleeding.

Tug Farrell found renewed strength as he topped the snowy slope and neared his horse. Though Raven Morrow and Clete Hobbs would never take the drop on a gallows, at least justice had been served. The sorrel nickered at its master as the lawman limped into view. Sliding the Winchester into the saddle boot, Farrell patted the animal's neck and said, "I hope you don't mind my getting into the saddle from the wrong side, boy, but I just can't lift this left leg to the stirrup." Pulling himself painfully into the saddle, using his hand to swing his leg over the horse's back, U.S. Marshal Tug Farrell said with a sigh, "Let's go, big fella. The war's finally over—and we've got a beautiful redhead and a freckle-faced little rascal waiting for us."

## THE BADGE: BOOK 16
## CANNON'S GRAVE
### by Bill Reno

When U.S. Marshal Josh Cannon is assigned to capture the bloodthirsty Emmett Kolfax, he knows he has a tough job. The gang leader is always masked, making it impossible for his victims to describe him —until a man shot and left for dead during a train robbery sees Kolfax's unmasked face.

While questioning the man, Cannon meets the victim's beautiful daughter, Dr. Trina Tabor, and his life takes on a new dimension as they fall in love. But they are soon separated when she is abducted by Kolfax and taken hostage. Cannon pursues the gang with a new fervor, and in a bizarre twist, Kolfax's men mistakenly believe they have gunned him down. Fearing retribution by other lawmen, Kolfax and his men retreat to the Hole-in-the-Wall, the notorious criminal hideout, and leave Trina in the hands of Kolfax's woman—along with orders to kill her young charge. Trina is devasted when she realizes that her captors have murdered the man she loves.

Trailing the gang to the Hole, Cannon masquerades as an outlaw and rides in. It is a race against time as he tries to win the trust of the men there, both to learn of Trina's whereabouts as well as to bring the Kolfax gang to justice. And if just one man in the Hole recognizes him, the masquerade will be over— along with Josh Cannon's life.

*Read* CANNON'S GRAVE, *on sale April 1990 wherever Bantam paperbacks are sold.*